> To Lizzie,
> You are
> of us all, may your
> carrots always be lovely!
> Love R.M. Gardner
> xo

Teach Me to live

STARGAZING SERIES, BOOK FIVE

R.M. GARDNER

ALL RIGHTS RESERVED

Teach Me To Live

Copyright © 2022 R.M. Gardner

No part of this book may be reproduced or transmitted in any form or by any means, electronic or mechanical, including photocopying, recording or by any information storage and retrieval system without the written permission of the author, except where permitted by law, aside from small quotations or excerpts to used in critical reviews and / or promotions.

This is a work of fiction. Names, characters, businesses, places, events and incidents are either the products of the author's imagination or used in a fictitious manner. Any resemblance to actual persons, living or dead, or actual events, is purely coincidental.

Collaboration Organiser: Phoenix Book Promo
Editing: Heather Ross
Cover design and interior graphics: Shower Of Schmidt Designs
Formatting: Phoenix Book Promo
Proofreading: Sam Brown

For my mum, Dianne. The strongest, most independent and loving person I know. I love you to the moon and back.

Please don't disown me if you read this.

Gemini

Gemini is traditionally represented by the twins and one of their strong traits is the fear of being alone.

Gemini women are said to be extremely passionate but can be scared of commitment as they are notoriously indecisive.

It is common for geminis to seek partners who can help them make sense of the chaotic emotions in their mind and can match them in their great intelligence and wit.

Teach Me to Live Synopsis

Teach Me to Live is book #5 of the Stargazing series, a 12 book series of standalones.

When Eren loses her the other half of her heart in a tragic accident, she's left to rebuild her life and live alone for the first time.

Eventually regaining power, she develops a new-found confidence, discovering she is competent, capable and able to stand on her own—an alien but exciting revelation.

Dylan meets Eren at the moment of her rebirth and wants nothing more than to get to know the beautiful, independent woman—to show her that love doesn't mean losing her identity.

When he goes through his own version of hell, he needs someone to lean on, turning to Eren, who gifts him her strength in an attempt to bring him back to life, too.

Will the pain of her past and his anguished reality cause their hearts to dim and despair to take over, or will the pair grow together in love and friendship despite all odds?

Prologue

20 years earlier

"Wait for me." My voice was high and breathless as I chased Edward up the hill. "It's not fair. My legs aren't as long as yours." I could hear him laughing as my little limbs pumped to within an inch of their lives.

He was so free when he was running. I always tried to keep up with him but it was always futile. He was so much more athletic than I was. He slowed down for me, as I'd known he would; he always did. He flopped down onto the grass, nestled amongst the buttercups, while I caught up and settled beside him, staying close. We were rarely more than a few metres apart—joined at the hip as our parents said. Teachers had tried to separate us in school but the tantrums and hysterics had very quickly shown them that it wasn't worth the hassle. We were a pair, a combo, our own little dream team. You couldn't have one without the other.

"What do you think mum will make for tea?"

"I don't know. I hope it's something big, though. I'm starving after all this running," Edward moaned, ruffling his mousy hair. No matter how much Mum combed and sprayed and gelled, Edward had a permanent bedhead. His mane could not be tamed. Mine was the same, curly and huge, but blonder than his. Our hair was the only physical feature that gave us away as twins. Otherwise, we were chalk and cheese. I had blue eyes and a small nose with full, pouty lips. He was my exact opposite. We'd asked our parents once if one of us had been adopted—you know, just in case—but apparently not. We just weren't identical.

"Well, this is why you should just walk with me," I complained, sticking out my bottom lip in a sulk.

"Come on, Eren. You know I won't leave you behind, never ever," he replied, and I believed him.

He gave me a piggyback ride back to the house. My pace was far too slow for his liking. Edward wanted to rush everywhere but I was more of a take in the view and smell the flowers kind of girl.

We opened the front door to the smell of rich gravy and minced meat cooking. I looked at my brother, my eyes lighting up. Cottage pie was our favourite and no one made it like Mum did. Dad had tried once when Mum had gone to visit her friend for the weekend. We'd got a pizza in the end because the mash and gravy both had lumps in, and half the mince had stayed stuck to the bottom of the pan.

"Wash your hands, please," our mother's voice bellowed from the kitchen.

"Then you can set the table for us," Dad's gruffer voice called out. We rolled our eyes in unison: like we needed telling. Setting the table had been our job for as long as we could remember. Mum cooked, Dad washed up and we did the inbetween. It was a good system because I loved making the table pretty. I would pick wildflowers from the surrounding fields to put in an old jam jar. I scoured car boot sales with Mum and spent my pocket money on table mats and doilies and the like. Family meal times were important to my Mum because it was something she never got to have as a little girl. TV dinners had been the staple of her single mum household. Grandma had worked two jobs and barely had time to make a sandwich, let alone sit down for a while to eat it.

It was Friday, which meant board games after tea. It was Edward's turn to decide on the game and we all knew what he would choose. The Game of Life was his favourite ever. He was obsessed with planning the future. He always said that when he grew up he would get married and have three children—two boys and a girl. They would live in a semi-detached house and the house it was attached to would be mine. We would have a gap in the garden fences so we could come and go as we pleased, and then when we got old we would retire and live together in an old folks home where his kids could come to visit us and his wife. He was also convinced I would be best friends with his wife.

"If she isn't good enough to be friends with my sister then she isn't good enough to be with me," he'd always said, his chin up and his arms crossed. I was the apple of Edward's eye and vice versa.

Some siblings drifted apart over time but we never did. Edward and I were always a team. We spent our whole adolescence and adult life together. We were together during primary school, high school, sixth form. We even shared a flat for the entirety of university. We were everything to each other and the thought of separating ourselves was beyond a joke. Even after university, our house together was our safe space. We could be ourselves; we could share our darkest fears, our wildest dreams and our deepest rooted insecurities. It was our home and we'd never even discussed the possibility of either of us moving out. In hindsight, we definitely should have discussed the concept but it just never occurred to us that we might have to live without each other one day.

Chapter One

The funeral was agonisingly slow. With a parent on either side, I glanced toward the coffin that held the other half of me.

I didn't cry.

I'd used up so many tears in the past two weeks that I felt wrung out. All I could do was stare at the coffin that held my brother. I knew that someone was speaking, telling stories about our childhood, about what he had achieved and what he had left behind.

"As we listen to our final piece of music, the

curtain will close, and we will say our final goodbyes to Edward."

Erm, no the fuck we would not. I wasn't ready to say goodbye. How could I be? How could I just walk out on my best friend of twenty seven years knowing that I would never see him again, never hear his voice again? I didn't hear what the song was. I just stared wide eyed at the box, willing it not to be real. My parents stood up and I knew that was my cue. My legs wobbled beneath me and the mahogany coffin grew blurry. Darkness edged my vision and my eyes slammed shut. I wasn't ready to leave him, but I didn't have a choice. I linked my fingers with my mum's and forced myself out of my seat. We left the room and the tears miraculously started up again. I couldn't stand the thought of leaving Edward there, but I did. I had to.

I couldn't bring myself to stay at the house Edward and I had shared, so I was back in my childhood bedroom, surrounded by old memories of our adventures. I dug out an old photo album and found the picture I was looking for...

We'd been nine years old and it was Halloween. We were trick or treating dressed up as Wednesday and

Pugsley Addams. I had the long black plaits and Edward had the stripey shirt and shorts. We had dark circles painted under our eyes and were grinning like there was no tomorrow, much more cheerful than the characters we were meant to be portraying.

We had gorged ourselves on chocolate that night until we'd both felt sick. We'd ended up sleeping in our parents' bed instead of our own and they had slept on the sofas in the living room. Whenever one of us was sick, the other one always looked after them. When we were both ill, we became the worst patients ever.

I crawled into my childhood bed with the photo propped up on the bedside table where I could see it. I had brought up the ridiculously unhealthy hot chocolate with cream and marshmallows that Mum had made for me and I sat under the covers, flicking on the television for some background noise. Growing up with a twin had been loud, and for the most part, silence made me very uncomfortable. I clutched my mug, enjoying the warmth in my hands, and scooped out some cream with my finger. The sugary goodness spread across my tongue and I closed my eyes, feeling more or less completely numb.

I woke up with a sore throat and puffy eyes. The dullness from earlier hadn't lasted long at all. The moment I tried to sleep, I was attacked by an onslaught of images of Edward, bruised and battered, lying helpless in the road, blood pooling at his head. I scrubbed my eyes, trying to banish the memory of that day, but it was no use. I was trapped. The visions brought with them violent sobs that wracked through my body. I stifled my cries with my pillow until I eventually exhausted myself and fell into a fitful sleep.

I was in no position to drag myself downstairs for breakfast with my family. I knew they needed my support but I was too wrapped up in my own misery to provide anything other than my presence. Instead, I crept to the bathroom, locking myself in for a bubble bath that I hoped would help ease the pounding in my head.

I took a book with me but it was wishful thinking that I would be able to lose myself in it. My ability to focus on anything other than the harsh reality I was living in was non-existent and had been since the accident. So, I spent two hours in the bath, staring at the wall, pleading with the universe to make today easier.

"Eren," I heard through the door. I let out a low sigh and put on my *everything's okay* voice.

"Yeah, Mum, what's up?"

"I've made you a tea. Do you want me to leave it in your room?" I sniffled, feeling guilty for closing myself off from her and Dad, but knowing that I had no help to offer them.

"Yeah, that'd be great thanks." I chewed at my lip, knowing I was being selfish. My parents had lost one child and here I was, their only daughter, hiding from them. I was a coward but I was terrified to face them.

In a way, things had felt easier before the funeral. Beforehand, we had something to look toward, a goal, a day that mattered. Now, there was nothing. Now, all we could do was watch each other struggle to go on with this new normal that had been thrust upon us. I wasn't ready to start this journey and the thought had my eyes stinging and my heart racing in my chest. I tapped my feet in a steady rhythm against the end of the bathtub and tried to match my breathing to it. I sank lower so my face was the only thing above the water's surface and let the muffled sound of my tapping wash over me and calm my nerves.

By the time I got out, my tea was cold but I drank it anyway, without really tasting it. I replaced the fluffy towel with my pyjamas and even fluffier dressing gown, which I tied tightly at the waist. The pressure felt comforting. I had no reason to get dressed. I was off work indefinitely and I was in no mood to leave my room, let alone the house.

We'd had a lot of visitors recently, people coming to check on us, offer their sympathies and occasionally bring us meals as a show of moral support. It had been exhausting entertaining so many guests but my parents were grateful for the distraction. Their grief was expressing itself in a very different way to mine. They had each other and they had experience on their side. I, on the other hand, was still young, and more alone than I had ever thought I would be.

I was trapped in a depression cycle: The depression made me feel sick. I felt sick, so I couldn't eat. I didn't eat, so I was always lethargic. I was always lethargic so I never left the house. I never left the house, so I was trapped inside my head with my memories of Edward. I was trapped in my memories, so I was constantly depressed. I was losing weight, rapidly. My parents were worried about me but their constant checking up was beginning to grate on me.

Chapter Two

After six weeks, I had already been driven to the point of distraction, so I left and went back to the home I had shared with my twin.

Mum had obviously been there. There was no fine layer of dust coating the surfaces, no cobwebs in the corners, no boarded up windows. My life had fallen apart and in a way, I had expected the house to fall with me. But everything was exactly the way we'd left it that day.

I walked past his room, my fingertips grazing along the pine door. I grasped the bronze handle, even turned it half way, but I couldn't go in. It was too soon. I knew that it would look the same but I was sure it would feel different. Even the hallway felt wrong, heavy somehow. Like the house knew that someone was missing, and that they weren't coming back.

My first night alone was spent in my bedroom. I may as well have stayed at my parents' house. My room and the bathroom were the only parts of the house I was used to being alone in and the clawfoot tub just wasn't as comfortable as my mattress. There was a forgotten bottle of red wine in one of the kitchen cupboards, so I took that to bed with me to watch cheesy romance films until my eyes couldn't stay open any more.

Sunrise brought with it a raging hangover and an immediate urge to vomit. I stumbled to the bathroom, stubbing my toe on the way and barely making it before spewing everything I'd ingested in the past twenty-four hours, which admittedly was just the wine. I lay down, exhausted, on the cool tiled floor. I needed to shower but my legs felt like jelly and I knew I was going to be horizontal for a while yet. I dragged a fresh towel down from the bathroom shelf to cover myself up with. I was a sweaty, shivering mess and there was no way in hell I was walking to my room and back to get the duvet.

The chill from the floor soothed the pounding in my head and I drifted in and out of sleep for another couple of hours before I was finally able to sit upright with my back against the wall. I eventually made it out of the bathroom and made a coffee, opting to leave the shower for a little while longer. Turning to find the television remote, I spotted it on the arm of Edward's chair and a lump formed in my throat. Wanting to feel some comfort, I sat in the armchair, my legs curled beneath me, and sank into the plushy fabric. It felt strange sitting there, but with a blanket over my knees, I found myself once again dozing off.

I woke up for the second time with my stomach grumbling. The television had put itself into standby mode and the dregs of coffee left in my cup had started to get that weird milk thing on the top. I stood and stretched, my back cracking like a glow stick, and shuffled to the fridge to look for food. I swung the door open and looked at the almost bare shelves. In my half asleep state, I hadn't considered the fact that I hadn't been here for some time. I thought back to the milk I'd used to make my coffee and realised Mum must have put it there for me. With a heavy sigh, I took it out to make another brew and cast a longing glance at the kitchen crap drawer, thinking about the take-away menus I knew were hiding in there. To buy food, or to make food? Buying food meant some form of human interaction but making whatever food I had stashed in the cupboards meant me actually doing something. I heard the click of the kettle and decided that I'd just order something to be delivered.

I rang in my order and went back to Edward's chair. I was pleasantly surprised by the comfort it gave me. I'd expected to feel nothing but pain being back in our shared home. I chugged my coffee then decided on a quick shower while waiting for my food. I washed my hair and enjoyed the feel of the hot water massaging my achy muscles. Sleeping on the bathroom floor and on the chair had done me no favours.

By the time the doorbell chimed, I was in fresh pyjamas with my hair halfway to being dry. I'd been in Edward's chair, watching *Friends*, my go-to entertainment. It played on a constant loop in our house; Ed had been just as big a fan as I was. I answered the door, and avoided eye contact with the delivery guy, thrusting my money out awkwardly and mumbling my thanks.

"Enjoy your food," he offered with a wink before walking away.

"You too," I stuttered, just loud enough for him to

hear. I heard a chuckle as he headed down the garden path and groaned as I realised what I'd just said. Apparently, my grief had the added side effect of taking away all my social skills.

Mum had rung me every day to check in, asking if I needed anything, telling me about different articles she'd read and what they said were the best ways to handle grief. It was lovely that she was trying to help me, but it wasn't working. All it did was make me feel like I wasn't grieving correctly. I wasn't constantly crying anymore. I wasn't cursing the world for the unfairness of it all. I was just numb.

It was different with Dad, though. Dad didn't probe or push me to feel a certain way. He didn't even ask me in too much depth about how I was feeling. He just sat on the couch, drank brews and watched the TV. A silent companion. It was perfect for me. I had taken up almost permanent residence on Ed's chair but sometimes I would sit on the sofa with my dad and lean against him. He would put his arm around me, still not saying a word, and I would feel comforted and protected. It was like being a teenager again, when I would argue with friends or break up with a boyfriend and go to my dad for hugs to make it all feel better.

It was during one of these moments when Dad admitted that Mum had sent him this time, to try to coax me out of the house for dinner with them.

"Just the three of us… Your mum's making a roast dinner," he told me, trying to gauge my response to the ambush.

I nibbled on my bottom lip. I hadn't left the house for anything other than shopping in the past few weeks. This would be my first social outing since the funeral.

"Your mum just wants to see you for a little while. You know how she worries," Dad explained. Guilt tugged in my chest at the thought of her stressing over me, and I nodded. I changed into a pair of leggings and my cosiest woolly jumper. I wanted to be comfortable if I was having to leave my safe haven.

Dad and I agreed that I would follow him in my car, so that I could leave whenever I was ready without having to wait around for anyone else. I walked into the familiar kitchen and I could feel the effort it was taking for my mum to hold back and give me my space. The look in her eyes made it clear that she was dying to grab me for a hug and never let go. I was determined not to push her away any more than I already had, so I went willingly towards her with my arms held out. She embraced me with extra strength that only a mum has, and I rested my head on her shoulder, shocking myself by enjoying the moment. I heard her sniffle but I didn't mention it. I was welling up, too, and I couldn't get a word out. I realised in that moment how much I'd missed her, that I really had been alienating myself since the accident.

Mum cleared her throat and withdrew from me, her hands going to my face. "You're looking a little peaky, sweetheart. Are you getting enough sun?"

I gave her a wobbly chuckle. "Probably not, but I'll try harder."

The oven timer began beeping and Mum rushed over, flapping about the vegetables. I went to the drawers with the intention of setting the table and froze when I realised what I'd done. Instinctively, I'd grabbed four of everything. My muscle memory obviously hadn't caught up to the fact that Edward was gone. I didn't want to upset Mum so I quickly left the room with the right amount of cutlery and scrubbed at my eyes with my free hand. I should've expected something like this to happen. In fact, it was a miracle that it hadn't happened sooner. In the back of my mind, all I could think was that this feeling wouldn't be here if I'd stayed hidden away at home.

Dinner hadn't been awful. It was awkward at times, but overall it could have been worse. We all tried to ignore the empty seat across from me but it may as well have had a neon *look here* sign flashing above it.

By the time I left I was completely drained. It had been a while since I'd had to make that much conversation with someone and it became evident very quickly that I had fallen out of practice. I contemplated that in bed that night, debating whether or not I was ready to go back to the office. Workwise, I was fine. I'd been working from home and nothing had suffered. It was my colleagues that worried me. They were all good people and would all be completely well meaning, but I didn't think I could cope with all of their pitying looks. You know the ones: *head tilt, then, "How are you doing, hon?"* Yeah, that one. I tried to convince myself that it would be good for me to go back and join the general population but my confidence was wobbly at best.

Chapter Three

I had been keeping in touch with my assistant, Angela, who had been a Godsend the whole time I'd been off work. Honestly, she could've done my job and hers if she'd wanted to. I mentioned that I was considering coming back to the office and we agreed to meet up for lunch first so that I could test out my boundaries with other people.

Getting ready to meet Angela made me realise how little I'd been taking care of myself. My hair had been in a messy bun for weeks. It was embarrassing how long it'd been since I'd used a hairbrush. I slathered on some conditioner and combed it through before rinsing to try to tame some of the tangles. I pulled out clump after clump of my curly blonde hair and with every tug I cried a little bit harder over the mess that I'd allowed myself to become. Looking in the mirror was hard. My eyes had sunk into my skull, my cheeks were hollowed out and I'd never known myself to be so pale. I'd become someone I didn't recognise, which brought on a whole new round of tears. Looking through my wardrobe, I settled on jeans and a t-shirt, both of which were too big, but it was the best I could do.

I set out to the coffee shop where we were meeting, avoiding glancing at myself in shop windows by keeping my gaze firmly on the pavement in front of me.

"Oof!"

I struggled to keep my balance and grabbed onto the outstretched hand in front of me. "Sorry," I mumbled. "I wasn't paying attention."

"No harm, no foul," said a male voice, rough and delicious. I glanced up at him and saw grey eyes framed with thick lashes and quickly scurried off without saying anything further.

I spotted Angela at one of the tables outside. When she saw me, her smile grew wide and she flashed a perfect row of teeth at me. I was relieved to see her and quickened my pace to join her at the little metal table.

"Eren, how have you been, my love?" she gushed, pulling me in for a hug. I relaxed into her embrace, finding that I'd missed being around her. I had always used the term assistant *very* loosely with Angela. I saw her firstly as a friend, and on a professional level I'd always considered her to be my peer.

"I'm okay. I've just been plodding along," I replied, my chin resting on her shoulder. "I'm better for seeing you, though."

"Well, of course you are. I'm great." She giggled, shaking her head, causing her tightly coiled hair to bounce around her face. "I've been wanting to visit you but I thought you might have needed your space," she explained, guilt flashing through her eyes as we sat down.

"No, you're fine, really. I've been looking like shit this whole time. I'm glad you didn't come and see that to be honest." She opened her mouth as if she was about to argue with me, but I cut her off before she could start. "Have you looked at the menu yet? I'm starved."

We made small talk while we waited for our meals to arrive. Heavy conversations couldn't be had on empty stomachs so we were half way through our food when she finally asked the question that had been on her mind.

"Are you sure coming back to the office is a good idea right now?"

I shrugged and worked on swallowing quickly so I could answer her. "I don't know. I feel like it's been a few months now. I should be ready, I guess."

"There's no expiration date on grief, Eren. You can take all the time you need." She reached across the table, covering my hand with hers, her dark skin in stark contrast to my own sun-starved milky white. When I started crying at her words, I realised that the timing still wasn't right. I was still too fragile.

"It feels like I'll never get out of this spiral, Ange. I'm stuck in this darkness and I can't get out." I pushed my half empty plate to one side and used my napkin to try to stem the flow of tears, not wanting to have a complete meltdown in public.

"You'll get out of it, but you need to give yourself time to heal. What you've been through, I wouldn't wish it on anyone. I think it's too early for you to come back to the office, but maybe you'd feel a bit better if you weren't constantly alone," she suggested, her voice maintaining its gentle resonance.

Angela had everything in the office under control, and me going back in that state would have just made things worse, so we agreed that I would carry on working from home for the time being.

After lunch, I remembered my mum's comments about not getting enough sun and decided to walk home the long way, thinking about what Angela had said about being alone all the time. She was completely right, of course. I had cut myself off from most people and I hadn't been the most sociable person to begin with.

I was strolling through the park when I saw a ball of fluff coming at me, followed by a woman trying to catch up. Instinctively, I bent down to scoop up the little dog before it could run any further and walked to meet their owner. The dog was like a little soot sprite—a black ball of fur with sparkling eyes and the tiniest little pink tongue hanging out of its mouth. I immediately fell in love with him.

"Thank you so much," the owner called as she jogged towards me. I was gutted to have to hand back the fuzzy little creature but of course, he needed to go home.

"No problem. What breed is he?" I asked, my interest piqued.

"He's a very naughty pomeranian," she told me, her eyes zeroing in on the little guy. "He ran out of the house. I don't know how I'm ever going to be able to sell this one"

That made my ears prick up. "He's for sale?"

"Yes, him and his siblings. I have their mum who was *also* very naughty and got pregnant before I could get her spayed." The lady smiled, clearly unable to stay mad about the issue. I leaned back in towards the pup and scratched him behind the ears.

"How much would a little guy like this go for?" I asked, trying to sound nonchalant but no doubt failing miserably.

"Only two hundred and thirty. I'm not looking to make any money from them. I just need to cover the costs I've spent vaccinating them. Are you interested?" She eyed me curiously.

Was I interested? Of course I was interested. He was absolutely gorgeous and even now he was wriggling around in his owner's arms trying to get back to me. But did I have time for a dog? I worked long hours, but I was also basically my own boss, so I could just take him with me to work when I eventually went back. He could run around my office with me, and we could go for walks on my lunch breaks. I'd get him toys and his own bed for the office. Besides, even Angela had said that I needed some company. I could do it. I made eye contact with the little guy and the decision was made.

"Yes, I'm interested. I would love to take him."

"Wow, that's great. I would like to know he's going to a good home, though. I'm sure you're lovely but I wouldn't feel right just passing him off to a stranger in a park." She nibbled on her bottom lip.

I smiled. "I understand. I only live up the road. You could come with me to check it out and ask me any questions you have," I suggested.

Chapter Four

Three hours later, I was the proud owner of Iggy. As soon as we'd entered my house and sat down, he had made himself comfortable on my lap and fallen asleep. Celia, his old owner, had exchanged numbers with me so she could check how he was doing and I could contact her if I had any issues, not that I foresaw us having any.

For our first afternoon together, Iggy and I went to the pet shop to get him properly kitted out to move in with me. I'd kept the lead Celia had clipped onto him when we met, so all we needed was food, bowls, a bed and some toys. I knew, as I was picking out the perfect bed for him, that it was an exercise in futility. As soon as Iggy's little face looked at me when I was in bed, I would let him up to snuggle but I thought I'd better at least pretend that wasn't going to happen. If nothing else, it would give him something nice to sit on in the car.

I worked at home for another few weeks—partially to potty train Iggy so we didn't have any accidents in the office, and partly to give myself some time to re-enter society instead of throwing myself in at the deep end. Angela came over twice a week to help ease my transition and my parents started coming around on Sundays, too, although I suspected that was more to see Iggy than me. I was doing better. I was looking after myself more, and I was getting out more. Having Iggy to focus on when I was down was helping. He needed my attention regardless of how I was feeling so I was forced to function, whether I wanted to or not.

After another month at home, I finally felt ready. I felt like I had a good enough grasp on my emotions to be able to function in the office like a normal human. I was nervous to go back but I figured once I was there, it would be like old times. The office was a place I could use to escape what I was facing at home. There were no reminders at work—no empty room to walk past, no mug sat next to the kettle waiting to be filled. All I had was what was mine.

Iggy went down a storm in the office when I went back in. I had ordered some cute bits and pieces on Friday so he entered the office on his first day in a tiny red tie and won everyone's hearts. I had to keep a careful eye on the jar of treats on my desk otherwise he would've had one every time someone came in. Angela spent most of the day finding excuses to come in and see us until eventually I told her to just bring her laptop in and work on the couch. I had an adorable bed delivered to the office so that Iggy could take a nap whenever he wanted. It was shaped like a teeny tiny arm-chair with a plushie cushion and a fluffy covering, and he had a selection of toys and chews to keep him entertained. Despite this, he spent the whole day alternating between mine and Angela's laps, and playing with the cardboard box his bed had arrived in.

I was still anxious about being back, but having Iggy and Angela around made it a lot easier. The odd person shot me a knowing look but no one brought up the tragedy that had befallen my family.

After the first week was done, I was finding it easier. But of course there came the inevitable downfall, and it came in the form of Gary—a well meaning but utterly tactless co-worker. Bless his heart, he was trying to help but that email set me back by weeks.

Hi guys,

It's been a while since we did anything. I was thinking maybe we should go out as a group and help Eren forget about Edward for a while?

Let me know!

Gary

Clearly, he hadn't meant for the email to come to me. He must have forgotten that I would get it when he hit *send to all*, which was why I never replied. That, and I was angry, but I didn't want to take that out on him. Don't get me wrong, part of me was angry at Gary. How could he even suggest that I "forget about Edward" even for one night? But he wasn't the only one I was angry at.

I was livid with Edward himself for leaving me like this. I knew it wasn't his fault. It's not like he'd got up that day with the intention of getting hit by a car, but I was still angry. I wanted him back here. He belonged with me and our parents. I was furious that he wouldn't be here to see the rest of our lives. I was angry for everything that could have been. I was angry with the hospital staff who hadn't been able to save him, the doctors and nurses who had tried their best but who hadn't been able to do anything more. I was angry with the guy driving the car even though it was an accident that he couldn't have predicted and couldn't have stopped. The poor guy was probably traumatised by that day and I was raging at him for what was essentially my brother's mistake because he was the one who tripped into oncoming traffic.

Finally, I was angry with myself—angry and disappointed. I was angry at myself for being angry at everyone else. I was angry at myself for not being able to help my parents because I was too busy feeling my own pain. And I was disappointed in myself, because I wasn't doing as well as I thought I should be.

So, Gary's email led to a panic attack and me running out of the office, clutching Iggy in my arms with tears streaming down my face and Angela chasing after me because in my state, I had forgotten my handbag, which had my house and car keys in it. I drove home and she followed me, her silver bonnet keeping steady in my rearview mirror. Once in the house, she made herself at home, making us both a brew and instructing me to go and change into my pyjamas. I didn't need much convincing because I was completely exhausted by the unexpected onslaught of emotions.

When I came back into the living room, Angela

was on the couch with her mug and a face that gave me big *we need to talk* vibes.

"I know, I'm crazy," I preempted, one hand buried in Iggy's fur for some comfort, the other holding my mug.

"You're not crazy. You're grieving," she told me, shaking her head at me. "Maybe you just need more time at home."

"No," I practically shouted. "I can't do that. I can't just keep staying here like a hermit. I'll never get any better if I do."

I was trembling, and I was at serious risk of scalding myself with my tea if I didn't calm down. "I just need to get my shit under control," I told Angela through gritted teeth.

Her thin brows knitted together in the middle and her bottom lip stuck out as she assessed me. "If you won't stay at home, would you at least consider coming to yoga with me?"

I was prepared for a further push towards me not working and was taken by surprise. "Yoga?"

"Yes, I go to yoga twice a week. It helps me keep a handle on my anxiety and means that I can eat more ice cream than I otherwise would." She winked. "It's all about controlling your breathing and clearing your mind. If you won't take more time off, I think this could really help you," she finished, her big brown eyes pleading with me to take her advice. I trusted Angela and knew that anything she suggested to me was because she genuinely believed it would help, so reluctantly, I agreed to try out the class.

Chapter Five

I'd been jittery all day from a combination of nerves and caffeine. I'd never done a yoga class before and I was terrified of making an absolute tit out of myself. Layla, my friend from way back when, was coming with us but she was so confident in everything that the thought of trying something new didn't faze her. I was hoping her conviction that it would go well would rub off on me.

Angela and I made the five minute drive to the

community centre straight from work and waited in the car park for Layla.

She finally arrived with a face like thunder, her candy floss pink hair dancing around her face in the wind.

"*Don't* get me started on my day," she warned as she linked arms with me and pulled me to the door. I had no intentions of getting her started but she didn't let my lack of questioning stop her from explaining. "I was doing this woman's hair and she said she wanted a fringe, so there I was snipping away, *chop chop-*" she made scissor motions with her free hand "-then just as I've done the first cut into the front of her hair, she screams at me to stop," she carried on. I wouldn't say I wasn't listening because that would be rude. I knew exactly what words were coming out of her mouth. I made the appropriate noises and Angela gave a good enough reply for both of us. I just didn't make an effort to keep the information in my head, that's all. By the time we reached the entrance, Layla had talked herself out about work and we had lapsed into a comfortable silence.

Walking into the hall, I felt an instant calm wash over me. The vibe from the other people was one of peace and tranquillity. The smell of lavender incense hit me and I could hear soothing piano music beneath the low buzz of conversation. Layla and I picked our places at the back to avoid any embarrassment as beginners, and Angela came with us.

We paid a middle aged, wise-looking woman and sat down as instructed to wait for the class to begin. She had a warm smile and kind eyes that made me think that she would be a great hugger. I expected the woman to be leading alone but she was joined at the front of the hall by a younger man. From the distance we were at, all I could see was that he was of average height and had dark hair.

The woman pulled her slightly greying hair into a ponytail and pulled off her oversized hoodie, showing off a fantastic figure in sports leggings and a vest top. If yoga would give me that look when I was her age I would be coming every week, forever! She introduced herself to the new members of the group as Flo and the gentleman beside her as Dylan, her younger brother. It seemed like yoga skills were a genetic gift in their family.

The class started with us lying on our backs with our eyes closed. I felt strangely vulnerable at first, despite the fact that everyone around me should have been in the exact same position. Flo's breathy voice instructed us to tense and relax our muscles from head to toe and I felt more at ease as soon as the sound of her voice reached me. She was soft spoken but confident. It was like she should be floating around making flower crowns but also like she would give you a swift headbutt if you crossed her. She came across as my kind of girl.

We were asked to sit up and Flo guided us through some simple stretches to warm us up. I was trying really hard and I was so focused, until I met a pair of storm cloud eyes across the room. Now, I didn't believe in love at first sight, but lust at first sight was a whole different story.

I immediately wanted him.

His very being called out to me. There was also a familiarity there that I just couldn't place. He held my gaze for what felt like forever until we were both pulled out of our trances when his sister said his name. "...and Dylan will be going around the room, helping you with your posture and balance while I demonstrate up here." Brilliant. I was already concerned about falling on my face but now I had to think about falling on my face *and* landing at his feet.

He stayed out of my way at first. I caught the occasional glance from him but he kept his distance. Maybe he could sense that he would make me nervous. Maybe my concentration face was scaring him off. I had been told on multiple occasions that I had a very severe case of resting bitch face.

We were doing well overall; neither myself nor Layla had ended up on our arses. It was clear that we weren't as flexible as some of the people there, but that was to be expected at first. Layla didn't look like she was enjoying herself, though, and the amount of times she yawned supported the theory. I, on the other hand, was having a lovely time and Angela kept grinning at me from her mat as she effortlessly slid into all sorts of weird and wonderful poses. I hadn't really exercised in goodness knew how long and it felt great to make my muscles work for once. I decided very quickly that I would be coming back.

It was during the transition from *warrior one* to *warrior two* that the inevitable happened and my yoga mat suddenly ended up very close to my face. I braced for impact but a strong arm caught me around my waist. For a brief millisecond I was suspended in the air like a ragdoll.

"Careful there, Goldilocks," an amused voice whispered in my ear. I suppressed a shiver as he set me back to rights. "Widen your stance," he instructed. "Arms out." He put his hands on me, one on my stomach and one on my back. "Tense your core and straighten up. Imagine pulling your belly button back to your spine."

I did as he said, but with great difficulty. I wanted nothing more than to melt into his hold and close my eyes, savouring the feel of him. But I didn't. I wasn't here for that. I was here for me and the reminder that I was here so that I could learn to turn off my mind and be comfortable living on my own was like a cold bucket of water being dumped over my head.

Chapter Six

After that first yoga session I started feeling better about myself. I'd had a couple of panic attacks since but between Iggy and the breathing exercises we'd used in class, I was able to calm myself down.

I had managed to conveniently sidestep the ill advised night out invitation from Gary. Yoga became a regular occurrence in my life, so Monday and Thursday nights were dedicated to working on myself and clearing my mind of anything else. It felt good to do something for me and I noticed that physically, I was feeling better, too. In fact, I was in the best shape of my life. It had been a fair few months since Edward had passed and while I still missed him every day, I was learning to enjoy living alone.

I had moved past the phase where I lay in bed, wondering what Edward would say if he could see me now. What he would think of me going back to work so soon, getting Iggy and maintaining my light relationship with my parents. The realisation that Edward's opinion was no longer relevant to my life hit me one night when I messaged Layla my concerns and thoughts and was met with a very firm but loving, "*Stop worrying about the opinion of someone who isn't here.*"

It was like a knife twisting in my heart but Layla's tough love helped me realise that I still had a life to live, even if my brother didn't. I had been forced to take charge of my life. I had transferred all the bills into my name alone, I had developed a little bit of a social life and things were on track with my parents. Iggy had taken centre stage in my universe and everything I did was either for him or me. I got myself to work, because I needed to be able to feed us both. I went out, because Iggy needed to go for walks. I took him to yoga with me, where he laid next to my mat with his favourite dinosaur teddy and watched as I attempted to contort myself into positions my joints felt were completely unnatural.

Overall, things were as good as I could have expected them to be. Angela and Layla had become friends in their mutual quest to get me back on my feet and I was grateful for that because they became my safety net. Although, I was slightly less grateful when they started ganging up on me to go on a night out.

I reluctantly agreed to go on what Angela referred to as *A Quiet One*. I distinctly remembered that the last *Quiet One* Angela had organised had led to her being hungover at work and vomiting in the staff toilets at lunch when she smelt someone else's pasta, so I was preparing myself for a somewhat messy night. We were getting ready together at my place and I was glad because if I'd been on my own, I would've completely chickened out and refused to leave the house.

We were all dolled up. Angela, with her hair pinned back, was wearing a short red dress and silver heels that made her toned legs look about six metres long. I was in a black bodysuit and a leather skirt, with knee high boots and my hair left to bounce naturally down my back. My hair was indisputably my best feature and I loved to let it do its own thing as much as possible. The hair Gods would take care of it much better than I ever could.

We queued for about half an hour to get into Angela's favourite club. By the time we entered, I was freezing and ready to go home again but the prospect of a gin and tonic was just too good to pass up on. Angela shouted at me that we should get a drink so we weaved, hand in hand, through the mass of sweaty, writhing bodies dancing between us and the bar. It had been a long time since I'd been out like this and I was completely out of my comfort zone. Luckily for me, Angela was in her element and she immediately propped herself onto the bar using her forearms, and shouted our order to the guy on the other side. I didn't pay much attention, focusing more on making sure that none of the people who were already bladdered got too close to me. We headed to a booth with our drinks when Angela let out a squeal and started bouncing up and down in place.

"Oh my God, Eren, it's my song!" I paused and cocked my head at her before it clicked what song was playing and realised that there was no way she was letting me off the dancefloor until Britney Spears had finished telling us just how much she really loved rock and roll. To tell the truth, I didn't mind too much. Of course, I made a show of huffing at her and shaking my head disapprovingly, but it was nice to be out and I was grateful to Angela for getting me to this point, so I indulged her and swayed and twirled with my gin in hand, until I spun into a familiar face.

I felt awful once I realised the dark patch on Dylan's t-shirt was because I'd just thrown half my drink at him, but I also couldn't help but admire how the t-shirt stuck to his chiselled abs and chest. He laughed immediately as I pulled a face of utter mortification at what I'd just done.

"Shit, Dylan, I'm so sorry. Let me get you a cloth," I started, feeling the heat rising up my face as I grew more and more flustered.

"Relax, Goldilocks. It was an accident," he assured me, meeting my frantic gaze with a look of sincerity. "Come on. Let's get you another drink."

I grabbed Angela's elbow as he put an arm round my shoulder and pulled me in the direction of the bar.

"Eren, where are we going?" she shouted over the bass thumping from the speakers.

I opened my mouth to respond but Dylan piped up first. "We're going to the bar. Eren just threw half a drink at me so I'm getting her another." He shrugged, like this happened every time he went out.

I scowled at him, half defensive, half amused, and turned back to Angela. "It was an accident. I didn't mean to." Dylan chuckled to himself and Angela flashed him a grin that both frustrated me and made me slightly jealous. I felt my mood dropping rapidly and pulled away from them both. "Actually, I think I'm good for another drink. Maybe I should go."

I thrust my half empty glass at Angela, hoping she would grab it, and turned to make a beeline for the exit when a big hand gently held my hip. I took a deep inhale, trying to calm the tremors I was beginning to feel, and schooled my face into a neutral position before I turned around. Dylan's hand dropped from my waist. He looked concerned, and a tad guilty. I was overcome with an urge to smooth out the lines between his brows with my thumb but I was nowhere near confident enough for that. Instead, I just stared at him, waiting for him to say something. Which, he didn't.

"Eren, you haven't even finished one drink," Angela yelled behind him, pulling my attention from Dylan's wide grey eyes. "Relax, babe. Remember, we're having fun," she urged.

I closed my eyes again and counted to ten in my head. "Okay..." I nodded. "Okay, I'll stay," I told her, deliberately not looking at Dylan in case his intense stare shook my resolve.

His gaze was thrilling and I had no idea what to do

with it. It gave me flutters in my stomach like nothing I'd ever felt before. It was different in class when we were in a controlled environment but here, we were basically in the wild and I had no clue what the rules were.

Angela handed me back my glass and said goodbye to Dylan before she tugged me to a booth in the back of the club where the music wasn't as imposing. She re-applied her lipstick while I tried to regain some semblance of calm. We didn't see Dylan again that night, but a drink was delivered to me by a barman from "that guy in the grey top" so we made an educated guess that it must have been him. Part of me wanted to see him again, to apologise and explain that I wasn't in the best place at the moment. But I knew that if he did reappear I would get tongue tied and panicky once more, so I let it go and hoped he wouldn't bring it up next time I saw him.

Chapter Seven

I made it home by ten o'clock that night, early for some, but for me, that was late. I lay in bed with Iggy, staring at the Halloween photo of Edward and I.

"You would've had fun tonight," I whispered into the dark. "You probably would've made me stay out for longer, though." I chuckled as a tear escaped my eye. Iggy licked the tear off my face and whined at me. I buried my face into his fur and closed my eyes. He made everything feel just a little bit easier. I turned the television on, not trusting myself to be alone with my thoughts, and propped myself up against the headboard with Iggy in the dip between my crossed legs. He rolled so he was belly up and let out a demanding yap, waiting for his evening tummy rub before we went to sleep.

Three films later, it was four am and I was still awake. My eyes burned and my brain ached but every time I got close to sleep, my body startled itself back to consciousness. Iggy had shuffled over to the side of the bed I wasn't occupying so I got up and tiptoed to the kitchen, trying not to wake him. Just as the kettle clicked to say it was done, I heard the telltale thumps of his paws sprinting down the stairs, telling me that he was awake and coming to find me. I squatted down, calling him over, and picked him up to snuggle while he licked at my ear, getting dangerously close to nibbling.

I put the fluff monster down to finish making my hot chocolate so he headed to the back door and scratched at it. I let him out to use the bathroom and sat on one of the metal chairs on the patio. I tilted my head back to look at the stars that glittered in the black velvet sky, and came close to spilling my second drink in one night when Iggy cannonballed onto my lap. It was chilly and the brisk night air was making me feel more tired than I already was, so I only lasted to the end of my hot drink, but it was a tranquil few minutes and when I got back in bed I fell asleep almost instantly, curled up around my little sooty bestie.

I woke up the next morning feeling good. Not great, still pretty tired actually, but good, especially considering I'd nearly had a meltdown the night before in front of a very hot guy and my very supportive co-worker. It was Saturday and I had the whole day to myself, so I got up and took my duvet down with me for a cosy day of being a couch potato and napping as and when I saw fit. I had just woken up from a nap with a stiff neck when my phone buzzed with a Facebook friend request and message:

Dylan: Hey, it was good to see you last night. Hope you enjoyed the rest of the evening :)

Oh. Well, that was a new development. I blinked a few times at my phone to make sure I wasn't seeing things before I typed back.

Eren: Yeah, you too. Sorry about your shirt.

Dylan: Like I said, don't worry about it. Hope you aren't too hungover today!

Eren: Not hungover, just tired. I was home by 10 but I couldn't sleep. What about you?

Dylan: I didn't drink enough to get hungover but I was out later than you, so yeah, I'm pretty tired too.

What the hell was I supposed to say to that? Come and nap with me? No, I think not! I wasn't proud of it, but I just left him on read. I had only just begun venturing back to the land of the living and my social skills weren't up for this. I would've loved to make some sort of flirty comeback but my brain just wasn't having it. I put my phone down on the table and went to get dressed to take Iggy out. I needed to stretch my legs and he was starting to do laps around the living room, a sure sign that he was getting restless. It was unseasonably warm so I opted for leggings and a thin cardigan with my trainers, which was a good choice because as soon as we reached the park, Iggy took off running, despite still being attached to his lead with me on the end of it.

I was sweating by the time he'd calmed down and slowed to a walk. Despite being in the best shape I'd ever been, I was apparently still wildly unhealthy by most people's standards. My cheeks were burning and I was panting, trying to catch my breath. Meanwhile, Iggy was sitting at my feet like butter wouldn't melt, looking at me with his onyx eyes and his pink tongue poking out between his teeth.

I narrowed my eyes at him and lifted him so he was at my eyeline. "You, little man, will be the death of me, won't you?" He yapped excitedly and licked the sweat off my forehead, not comprehending the fact that he had done anything even remotely wrong and there was no way I was going to be able to stay mad at him for long enough for him to figure it out. By the time we got back home, I was completely shattered and my stomach was rumbling.

Chapter Eight

Layla came over for tea—well, partially for tea, partially to see Iggy. Since getting a dog, my friends had suddenly become a lot more interested in hanging out at my house rather than in pubs and clubs. I had no energy to cook anything major, but being the heroine that she was, Layla's mum had sent leftover pie and I had frozen chips in the oven. I could tell from her face that Layla was dying to ask me something, but I didn't ask and counted down the minutes until she finally said what was on her mind. She lasted eight minutes.

"So, how was your night out?" she asked, her voice coy and inviting.

"Not bad." I shrugged. "I didn't have it in me to stay out long."

She frowned at me, clearly hoping for a better answer. "Did Angela have fun?" she pushed.

"Seemed to," I said. "We bumped into Dylan—you know, the guy from yoga?"

"The hot one?" she asked, perking up immediately.

"Sure, if you're into that."

"Tall, muscular and handsome—you're not into that?" she questioned, incredulous.

"Well, I didn't say that. But I made a complete idiot of myself, chucked a drink on him and nearly had a meltdown in the middle of the club, so I don't think it really matters whether I'm into him or not," I snapped, frustrated that she was pushing this line of questioning.

Layla rolled her eyes at me and continued to fuss over Iggy.

"Alright, mardy arse, calm down. I was only asking." I instantly felt bad. I was on the defensive and she didn't deserve my attitude.

I flopped down into Edward's chair, running my

fingers over the fabric and counting my breaths. "Sorry, that was bitchy. I just meant, yeah alright he is hot..."

"More than hot," she corrected.

"More than hot," I agreed. "But I'm a mess right now."

Layla assessed me, her head tilted to one side, and I knew she was thinking her next words over before they came out of her mouth.

"How long are you going to keep acting like you're a mess?"

I felt my jaw drop and my hands curled into fists on the arms of the chair. "Excuse me?"

"How long are you going to keep avoiding things because you're *a mess*?" she asked, one perfectly plucked eyebrow raised.

How dare she? How dare she act like I was using Edward as an excuse not to do things?

"I *am* a mess. I can't do *anything* right now!" I fumed, my voice rising in volume as I went on.

"Really? Because to me, it looks like you're taking care of yourself here pretty well," Layla argued, her chin up in defiance.

"Get out," I forced through gritted teeth. "Get the fuck out of my house, Layla. How dare you suggest I'm not grieving my brother?"

"Eren, that's not what I-"

"OUT!"

The pie was still heating up when I kicked Layla out of my house, but I was so livid that I just binned it and had chips and gravy for tea. I knew it was petty but honestly, fuck her. She had no idea what I was going through. She was an only child so she would never understand the bond Edward and I had had, or how hard it had been to lose him. She didn't know how many times I'd cried myself to sleep, how often I still talked to him as if he would talk back. She had no idea that I still couldn't bring myself to go into his room. Who the hell did she think she was?

All of these thoughts somehow made their way out of my mouth in between chips, and Iggy looked at me with doleful eyes that shone with sympathy. So what if I was doing better? *Ooh, I can go to work every day now. That must mean I'm over it then*! Urgh.

Iggy trotted around the house after me as I stomped about looking for my yoga mat, and his noises of encouragement spurred me on to say everything I had been holding in over the last few months. I was done trying to talk to other people who didn't get it, so talking to myself was my only other option. I finally found my mat by the front door after walking past it three times, and rolled it out. I took a deep inhale like

Flo had taught me and tried to clear my mind before bending into *mountain pose*. I tried to exhale all of my negativity and inhale only good vibes, which was made a lot easier by Iggy lying at the end of the mat watching me. By the time I was finished, I was almost as calm as I had been that morning.

Chapter Nine

Layla tried to reach me over the next few days but I wasn't ready to speak to her. I knew that if I responded, I would just do a lot of shouting and nothing would get resolved, so I left it. Dylan had been back in touch, too, and I was tentatively responding, trying to form some kind of friendship at the very least. By the time I went back to yoga on Tuesday, I was confident enough to say hello to him when he came around the room, and I was rewarded with a blinding smile that left me dazed. We continued to talk online, never anything heavy, just asking how the other one was, what we were up to and whether or not we would be at yoga. I got bolder and bolder each time I saw him, until I got to the point where I was staying after class just to talk to him and have him walk me out to my car.

"So, what do you do when you're not here?" Dylan asked one day as I rolled up my yoga mat.

"Oh..." I fumbled with my things. "I work at a marketing company,"

"Hey, Flo, did you hear that?" he called to his sister. "Goldie here does marketing. Maybe she can help you out."

Oh. So he wasn't actually interested in me like I'd thought. This was a networking opportunity. I shouldn't have complained, because networking was really important in my line of work; I'd just hoped that maybe we had been building up to more than that. Flo was making her way over to me so I plastered a smile across my face despite my disappointment.

"Is that so?" she asked in a butter wouldn't melt voice.

"I do. I work at a small but... diverse company," I explained. "Are you looking for some help in the marketing department?"

"Oh, you sweetie. I am, but I'm sure I couldn't afford someone like you." She grimaced. I shuffled in my duffle bag and found one of my cards.

"Have a think about what you need and then give me a call. You can come and see me at home for an informal chat between friends and I'm sure we'll be able to work something out." I smiled gently. I knew all too well how hard it was to get your name out as a small business. When I had first started working at Mantis Marketing, it had been an even smaller organisation and I'd been one of the first to join so we'd worked hard on getting word out about ourselves. If I could help Flo in any way, I absolutely would. Her yoga classes had given me so much after all.

Chapter Ten

Iggy's yapping alerted me to the imminent knock on the door that I had been waiting for. Flo and Dylan had arrived to talk shop and I had just put the spaghetti on the hob.

"Hi," I greeted them, opening the door to let them in. Dylan held out a bottle of red wine and Flo had brought a bunch of sunflowers. I had said they didn't need to bring anything but clearly they hadn't listened. I graciously accepted their gifts and poured them some wine at the table.

"Wow, Goldie, this chorizo is so good," Dylan gushed.

I felt my cheeks heating up and hoped they'd put it down to me being flustered in the kitchen. "Thanks, it's just normal meatballs and bolognese but I fry the chorizo in red wine before putting it all together," I told him. It was one of my signature dishes. I didn't have many excuses to make big meals for multiple people nowadays so I had taken advantage when the opportunity had been handed to me.

After dinner, we stayed at the table to discuss exactly what Flo needed from me. I had gone full marketing geek and had my A3 pad, pencil case, laptop and notebook out so that we could jot down every idea we came up with.

"Well, to be honest, I don't really know where to start." She sighed, looking to her brother for help.

"Okay, let's start with the basics. Do you have a logo?" I prompted.

"No."

"Do you have an idea of what you want for a logo?"

"No." She smiled nervously.

I grabbed my pad and pencil, ready to start doodling. "Okay, so the name is Flow with Flo. What does that make you think of?"

"I don't know." She shook her head, nibbling at her bottom lip. "Just me and yoga, I guess."

Dylan rolled his eyes with an affectionate smile. "I think of water," he suggested, coming to his sister's rescue.

I thought about that for a minute. "What if the name is just *Flow*? Then we could do your branding to look like a body of water."

The pair looked at each other and I saw Flo's eyes gleaming. "It could be like the river we used to camp out by," she whispered.

A conspiratorial grin spread over Dylan's face. A fleeting moment of sadness swept over me. That was the way Edward and I had been, all inside jokes and shared memories. Watching it made me miss him even more. I was doing better at being on my own but every now and then I had these moments where my independence felt more like loneliness.

As if he was aware of the dent in my armour, Iggy pawed at my thigh, demanding to be brought up for attention. By the time he was settled on the chair next to me, Dylan and Flo had suggested that they find some pictures of the river to inspire me.

I pulled up all of the packages I had to offer: posters, business cards, online adverts, radio jingles. Anything you could think of to promote a business, I could do. Dylan was nodding along with me as I explained the pros and cons of each option, but I saw Flo's face drop like a lead balloon. I tilted my head as I watched her, trying to figure out at what point I'd said something she didn't like but I didn't need to look for long.

"Eren, this is all amazing." She shook her head. "But there is no way that all of this is in my price range," she finished with a grimace.

I snapped my laptop shut and fixed her with my sternest stare. "I haven't told you about my prices."

"I know, but..." She trailed off, guilt flashing over her face.

Dylan gave me a knowing look and elbowed his sheepish looking sister. "I looked your company up online and I can barely afford two hours of your time, let alone anything else."

I could see in her face that this was something that had been bothering her. There was an element of shame in her expression, but also relief that she'd gotten it off her chest.

"Dylan, can you do me a favour? There's another bottle of wine in the fridge. Would you mind grabbing it for me?" I smiled sweetly and batted my eyelashes the teensiest bit. He got up from his seat with a lazy smirk and squeezed my shoulder as he passed. I shivered at his touch and the heat from his hand lingered, but I knew I had to put my butterflies aside to deal with the matter at hand.

"Okay, Flo, here's the thing: we're doing this at my house and you are a personal friend as far as I'm concerned. This isn't a paid job," I explained, reaching my hand across the table to her. "This is just a favour."

"Eren, I can't-"

"I'm not asking. I'm telling you. You and your yoga have helped me so much recently. I've been able to branch out, make friends and keep myself going. Now I can help you. Fair is fair."

Dylan came back in with the fresh bottle and clocked us having a moment. I felt his presence behind me but I chose not to acknowledge him, focusing on Flo. Her eyes left mine to meet her brother's and I saw the ghost of a smile on her thin lips.

"Okay," she croaked, coming back to me. "I'm in."

Dylan poured everyone a fresh glass, as if I wasn't supposed to be the one hosting, and I found I quite enjoyed his attention. Of course, I had fancied him since I'd first set eyes on him. His mysterious grey eyes, that designer stubble that was always at a perfect length, the fresh out of bed hair and of course, the abs that were sculpted by the Gods themselves. But here, in the comfort of my own home, I felt something new. Something more… wholesome.

After a couple more glasses of wine, Flo ordered her taxi. Dylan had, at some point during the evening, ended up sitting next to me. Iggy had settled himself on Dylan's lap and his arm was around the back of my chair. Once his sister had gone home, Dylan and I stayed at the table. The alcohol in my system had me feeling more confident than usual and clearly he was feeling the same way.

"So, Eren, you live here on your own?" I cleared my throat. I'd known that as our friendship grew, at some point he would eventually ask more personal questions but I hadn't expected it there and then.

"Yeah, my twin brother used to live here with me but he's, um… He's passed away now." I closed my eyes briefly in an attempt to hold back the moisture that I could feel welling up there.

"Shit, I'm so sorry. I didn't realise," he started, his hand coming to rest on my leg.

"It's fine," I sniffled. "It's just a bit raw. It's only been a few months since it happened."

"Was it unexpected?"

"Very. We were walking home from a night out. He tripped over, fell off the curb and got hit by a car," I choked out. In my head I was going to tell Dylan that

I didn't want to talk about it but the story had just fallen out of my mouth. All the conversations we'd had together had shoved me further into being comfortable with him and now I was paying for it. He was going to see how messed up I really was and we would go back to being acquaintances, because why would he want to get involved in something like this?

Dylan didn't ask me any further heavy questions. Mostly, he just told me about himself, sensing that I wasn't really in a position to talk about my life. He told me about his relationship with Flo, how he helped her with her yoga business but that he was actually a labourer by trade. His mum had passed away years ago but his dad was alive and kicking, having retired to Cyprus. By the time Dylan left, I was feeling better again and it was nice to know more about him. I walked him to the door, and before leaving, he pulled me in for a hug.

"I'll see you soon, yeah?" he whispered into my hair.

"Yeah, soon," I promised, and I thought I felt something on the crown of my head but I must have imagined it.

I slept well that night, feeling slightly more like my old self.

Chapter Eleven

I was working hard for Flo in between my usual work, yoga and Iggy. It was tiring, but it was worth it. I felt like I was doing something worthwhile, like I was somehow paying her back for all the help her classes had given me. Of course, I knew that it was in no way the same, but it felt good to give a little something back.

I'd arranged to stay after yoga to show Flo what I'd come up with so far. Dylan was there, too, with photos of the river for me. He thrust the photos into my hand

and subtly slid his other arm around my waist while I was chatting with Flo about business card fonts. I use the term *subtly* lightly because in actual fact it was very obvious what he was doing, but I didn't mind. I enjoyed the attention he gave me. It made me feel good about myself and I was doing a good job of not reading too much into it. After all, we hadn't actually talked about it. We just acted in a way that felt natural.

I flicked through the pictures at home and found myself reminiscing about Edward and our childhood together. The river looked beautiful. There were photos of it from every season and it reminded me of the pond we'd had in the back garden growing up. There were no fish in it or anything; it was just there. We were always told to stay away from it, and there had been a fence around it when we were really small to stop us from accidentally falling in. As we got older, it became the place we went to have secret discussions, and a lot of our make-believe games centred around it. We would pretend that a troll lived at the bottom of it that wanted to eat us, or that it was a magic pond that if you threw money in you could make a wish. That's how Dad had lost a tenner once. He wasn't happy and Edward had been grounded for a week, which meant that I'd stayed in for a week, too, because where would I ever go without him?

I photocopied the pictures and uploaded them to my laptop so that I could give the originals back as soon as possible, and sat at the table to begin my designs for the logo. In all of the pictures, I spotted the same willow tree that I wanted to work into the logo so I used that as my jumping off point. Iggy was a good boy while I worked. He climbed up onto the table next to my sketchpad and curled up for a nap, placing himself so he was close enough to be stroked at regular intervals. I was absorbed in my work, using water-colour pencils to create the perfect, soft atmosphere that a yoga business needed and blending the colours to create something that would still stand out from the crowd.

I worked for so long that my back was in agony from being hunched over my sketchpad. I limped my way to the bathroom, glad that I had taken Iggy out before I'd started working, and ran myself a hot bubble bath. Thank God for muscle-soak bubble bath. While I waited for the bath to fill, I fired a text to Flo to let her know I had some ideas for her to review and checked my work emails to see if anything had come in. I was a slight workaholic so out of hours didn't really mean anything to me. It was past ten o'clock at night so I wasn't expecting Flo to reply to me until the following day, but my phone pinged anyway and I glanced at it out of curiosity. It was my mum.

Mum: Hi Sweetie, I saw Layla today and she said you weren't talking. Is everything okay? X

I huffed and rolled my eyes before texting back.

Eren: Yep, all good. She just upset me, that's all. I'll talk to her when I'm ready. X

I knew Mum was just trying to make sure I was okay, but I really wasn't in the mood to have to go through the whole thing with her so I tried my best to tell her to leave it without really saying it.

I knew I needed to talk to Layla, and knew that I needed to do it sooner rather than later. I really didn't want to lose her friendship over this, but I also wanted to make it clear that what she had said to me wasn't okay and that I would stand up for myself. I adored Layla but she could be pushy and sometimes she needed to be put in her place. I reasoned with myself that it was too late in the day to do anything now, but that I would message her tomorrow and see how it went from there.

I lay back in the hot water and let it work its magic on my sore muscles, with my phone on the shelf playing an audiobook. The narrator's voice was rough but soothing, and it reminded me of a certain grey-eyed man. I closed my eyes and the sound washed over me. I didn't pay attention to what was being said. I just enjoyed the voice and let it combine with the room's aura to lull me into a state of restfulness.

I must have dozed off in the bath because I suddenly felt very cold and my toes had gone all pruney in the water. I got out, wrapped myself in a towel and ran across the hall to my bedroom where Iggy was waiting, sprawled out on my side of the bed like he owned the damn thing. I put my pyjamas on and got under the duvet, picking Iggy up and replacing him on the other side of the mattress. He was a funny little thing who craved being close to people, so within seconds he was tucked in against my side, his head resting on my hip. His presence was comforting and I fell asleep again in record time.

I went to work the next day feeling good. Iggy was tottering around the office with his favourite panda teddy in his mouth, showing it to anyone who happened to come by, and I had reached out to Layla and asked her if she wanted to meet up for lunch so we could talk. I had cleared my afternoon for a meeting with a big client but they had cancelled, so after my lunch date I was free as a bird.

Chapter Twelve

Layla and I had agreed that we should take advantage of the weather, so we found a beer garden to sit in where Iggy could soak up the sun and we could have a glass of wine with lunch to take the edge off. We ordered and Layla launched into an apology as soon as the waiter left the table.

"I'm so sorry, Eren. I swear I didn't mean to upset you. It just came out the wrong way. I've been feeling awful about it ever since and I wanted to come over and explain myself but then I thought you would want to be left alone and-"

"Stop, Layla," I interrupted. "It's not just you. I'm sorry, too. I should've handled it better. It just upset me when you said I was doing fine because I wasn't. I'm doing better now but at the time I felt like I was still constantly on the verge of a meltdown and I felt like you were trying to downplay what I was feeling," I explained gently.

"I completely see what you mean, and that was never my intention. I just wanted to encourage you," she promised. We hugged it out, like I knew we would, and all was right in our little bubble again. I was glad it was resolved because I'd missed my friend.

Layla was a little tipsy by the time we left but I'd stuck to the one drink, knowing that I had to walk Iggy and go to yoga yet. Iggy's walk consisted of getting from the beer garden, back to our house. Angela had given me a lift to work in the morning so I didn't need to worry about the car, and by the time we got back I was more than ready to call it a day and have a nap. So I did.

Chapter Thirteen

My alarm went off an hour before I needed to be at yoga, so I had a chance to have a sandwich and a brew before leaving the house. Iggy was a little more restless than usual so he went to visit the other people in the class and watch them, leaving me to myself. I jumped out of my skin when his cold nose poked my cheek as we were winding down at the end, and I heard Dylan laughing not far away. I expected him to come and chat while I was sorting myself out to leave, but Flo got to me first.

I didn't miss the look of frustration that flashed across Dylan's face when he turned away from us and walked back up to the front.

"Hi, Eren, I got your text last night," she told me, bending down to pick up Iggy who immediately decided she needed a hundred kisses. "Do you want to come to dinner at some point and we can look over what you've got? Or would you prefer to do it at yours again?"

"Whichever is best for you," I assured her. "I'm not fussy. I'll just need to know beforehand if I'm taking Iggy to my parents for the evening."

"Oh, don't worry about that. Iggy can come, too, can't you, my little darling?" she cooed, smothering his little head in kisses as he wriggled in her arms, his tail wagging a mile a minute. "I've got a manic few weeks but maybe a Saturday next month?"

We agreed the date and I set off to leave, but Dylan caught me just before I reached my car.

"Eren, wait," he called, jogging towards me. "I wanted to ask you something."

"What's up?" I asked, putting my stuff on the back seat. I turned around and if I'd been a more confident woman I would have assumed he'd just been ogling my arse.

"I wanted to ask whether maybe you might want

to go on a date with me?" My face must have changed because his eyes widened and he started to backtrack. "It's fine if not. Don't worry about offending me."

"No, no, it's not that. I do want to," I reassured him. "I just wasn't expecting you to say that," I admitted, suddenly feeling shy like I had when we'd first met.

"Great, so I'll pick you up at eight tomorrow night?" he suggested.

"Sure, see you then." I smiled and he surprised me again by leaning in and pressing a peck on my cheek before he jogged back into the building.

I drove home completely bemused and slightly nervous for what tomorrow would bring.

It had been a long time since I'd been on a date. I'd only really dated when I was at university because as soon as I'd left, I'd thrown myself into my work and had no time for a love life. Now that I was comfortable in my place at the agency, I had time for these things but I hadn't expected that the first date I went on would be with someone that I actually fancied so much.

My stomach was in knots. I had thirty minutes before Dylan was picking me up and I was standing in a bra and knickers with no idea what to wear. It was unseasonably chilly, so I wanted something warm, but my jeans all felt too casual and I couldn't find my favourite sweater. I decided I wasn't going about five times before I just grabbed a black dress and a red blazer, and called it a day out of sheer desperation. I was just putting the finishing touches on my hair when Iggy started yapping and I heard a car door slam shut outside. I smeared on my lipstick and hurried to the door. With one last glance in the hallway mirror, I was ready.

Chapter Fourteen

I wasn't ready.

As soon as I opened the door, my palms started to sweat and I could feel my knees wobbling. I fought the urge to wipe my hands on my dress and gawped at him like an idiot, but he didn't seem to notice.

"*Wow*, you look stunning," he told me, his frame filling the doorway. I stuttered out my thanks and turned to Iggy to give myself a moment to calm down.

"Iggy, be a good boy. I'll be home soon." I put him

on the sofa after kissing him on his perfect, fluffy little forehead. "Love you."

Dylan sniggered behind me but I ignored him. Why wouldn't I say goodbye to my dog before I left? He needed to be told I was coming back!

"So," I started, locking the front door. "Where are you taking me tonight?" I was still nervous and couldn't handle the quiet.

"We are going to Buon Cibo," he told me, opening the car door for me like a gentleman. "And then, depending on how we feel, I was thinking we could go for a drink somewhere." He shrugged, as I clicked my seatbelt into place. My eyes tracked his figure as he walked around to his side of the car and I could feel the tension leaving my body in his presence.

I turned to face him as he was about to set off. "You know, you look pretty good yourself."

He smirked and squeezed my thigh. "Thanks, babe."

We pulled up and once again, Dylan opened my door for me. I could definitely get used to that. He put his arm around my shoulders and tucked me into his side as we walked into the restaurant, and I felt safe and protected in his hold. I was slightly disappointed when we got to our table because it meant he let me go so I could sit down.

We were placed in an intimate corner of the room, which suited me just fine. The dimmed lights and candles on the tables gave the whole place a romantic atmosphere. The waiter pulled out the chairs for us, took my coat and moved to tuck me in. I noticed him looking me up and down when he thought my attention was elsewhere. I also noticed that Dylan was glaring at the offending man and before I knew it, he was by my side, his hand on the back of my chair.

"I've got it, man, thanks," he deadpanned, clearly marking his territory. I couldn't say I minded. The idea of Dylan getting jealous and being possessive over me made the butterflies in my stomach come to life.

I relaxed in the velvet covered seat and tried my hardest to look sophisticated and demure, as if this man hadn't already seen me in a t-shirt and gym leggings with no make-up and day three hair. We ordered drinks and perused the menu.

Usually, when going out I would have looked at the menu online ahead of time but as I'd had no warning, I was trying to consider my options as quickly as possible without ignoring Dylan in the process. I settled on lemon risotto and set my menu aside. Dylan was still looking and I took advantage of this to really take him in. He was in a crisp white shirt that stretched over his pecs and was tight around his biceps. He had shoulders that I wanted to run my hands over, and his hot chocolate hair had the same effect on me. I took a drink, just so I had something to do other than drool over him. I had seen him before, obviously, but I'd never really *looked* at him like this. He was just ridiculously delicious.

"So..." He looked up from his menu and caught me staring. "See anything you like?" *Oh fuck yeah.* "I heard the chicken pomodoro here is amazing."

"I'm gonna go for the lemon risotto," I told him as the waiter arrived. The poor guy barely looked at me after Dylan's earlier display.

We made small talk until our food arrived and I was able to relax into the light chatter with him. We discussed our families: he and Flo were the only children their parents had, and unfortunately they had lost their mother when Dylan was ten. Their dad had retired to Cyprus a couple of years ago with a lady friend and came home to visit once a year. They seemed like a solid family unit and I enjoyed hearing about Dylan and Flo's exploits.

I didn't say much about my family but there wasn't really much to say these days. Now that it was just my parents and I, we were a fairly boring bunch. Edward had always been the adventurous one, whereas I was a definite homebird. We opted to share a dessert and it was the correct choice because when the cheesecake arrived, it was a huge slice. I could only manage a few forkfuls before I had to abandon Dylan to finish it by himself. Otherwise, I was going to burst out of my dress.

When the bill arrived, I reached for it and got there just before Dylan, who shot me a quizzical look over the table.

"Let me get this," I tried, but he was already shaking his head before I'd even finished.

"Not a chance. Let me be a gentleman." I chewed my lip, not liking the thought of someone else paying for me.

"At least split it with me?" I asked, looking at him through my lashes, trying to butter him up to the idea. He weighed up his options and eventually let me pay for dessert. I was glad that he hadn't put up too much of a fight. I didn't want this to start with the idea of me not being able to take care of myself. I might have been being slightly dramatic but oh well. It was what it was.

"So what now?" he asked as we left the restaurant, his hand on the bottom of my back.

"We could have that drink," I suggested. "Maybe back at my place?" He raised an eyebrow in a cheeky way and my cheeks heated as I realised how my suggestion sounded. "Just because I don't like to leave Iggy alone for too long," I hurried out, not wanting to lead him on.

"Relax, babe," he chuckled, touching his forehead to my temple. "I'm not expecting anything," he assured me and I relaxed in his hold, giggling to myself. This man made me stupid. Literally, all brain cells bar one left my body whenever he was nearby.

When we walked through the front door, Iggy barrelled towards us and Dylan bent down to grab him. His teeny legs were flapping about in the air and Dylan was lucky he didn't get Iggy's tongue up his nose given how excited the little guy was. I laughed to myself and slipped off my shoes, padding barefoot to the kitchen to grab drinks.

"Wine?" I called behind me to Dylan, thinking he was still in the hallway.

I felt strong arms coming around my waist and his chin rested on my shoulder as he whispered, "Wine sounds great."

I suppressed a shiver and reached into the cupboard at my head for glasses. I turned in his arms after putting the glasses beside us and came face to face with him. His eyes burned into me and I watched as he took in my face, paying particular attention to my lips. My mouth went dry as I stared back at him, trying to assess what his next move would be. I hoped that he would kiss me. I was desperate to know how he tasted, how his lips would feel against mine. I was nearly brave enough to close the gap between us, nearly. But he moved first and tilted his forehead to touch mine, nose to nose. I closed my eyes and inhaled his scent. He smelled incredible—like a winter morning, fresh and enticing.

"Dylan," I whispered, tilting my head to the side.

His stormcloud eyes snapped open. "Yeah, babe?"

"How long do I have to wait for you to kiss me?"

Immediately, one of his hands moved from my waist to my hair. He pulled my body flush to his and brought our lips together. They were as soft as they looked and my tongue poked out to lick them. He groaned into my mouth and I ate it up, letting his tongue caress mine. He tasted like spearmint gum and I couldn't get enough of him. He lifted me up and sat me on the kitchen worktop. My legs opened on instinct to let him in. I gripped his shoulders as he kissed up my neck. It felt delicious as he nipped across my collarbone and I threw my head back, eager to grant him better access.

CRACK!

"Oh my God, Eren, are you okay?" Dylan gasped, his face full of concern. Both his hands flew to the back of my head, our intimate moment forgotten as he tried to assess how much damage I'd done when I bounced my head off the cupboard door behind me. His fingers found the rapidly rising fleshy bump and I winced involuntarily.

"Shit, babe, I'm so sorry," he whispered, lifting me back off the counter. I expected him to put me down on the floor but he carried me to the couch. "Wait there. I'll get you something cold for it."

Iggy immediately joined me on the couch, licking my face and fussing over me. Dylan hurried back with a bag of frozen peas wrapped in a tea towel and knelt on the floor beside me. I pressed the peas to the bump and jumped at the cold.

"Are you okay? Do you feel sick or-"

"Dylan, relax, I'm fine. It's just a bump," I assured him.

"Are you sure? It sounded painful."

"I'm sure," I told him, caressing his cheek. "Come and sit on the couch with me," I urged, patting the cushion my feet were on.

He carefully lifted my legs and sat, letting me rest my feet on him. "Sorry I killed the mood," I chuckled, shaking my head at my own idiocy.

"Don't be ridiculous. We had a great night, didn't we?" I detected a hint of insecurity in his voice and I jumped to erase it.

"We had an amazing night, thank you." I smiled at him and rested my head on the couch cushions. Iggy started snoring on my chest and Dylan took it upon himself to rub my feet. I let out a soft sigh as his thumb rubbed up the arch of my foot. It felt so good after being in heels all night.

I stretched to grab the television remote off the coffee table and flicked on a music channel for some ambiance. It said a lot to me that we were able to sit like that, without talking but still comfortable in each other's presence. I'd never been able to do that with a man before. The connection we had made my heart sing.

It was past midnight by the time Dylan left. He wanted to be sure that he wasn't leaving me with a concussion. We had decided against another drink just to be safe. I wasn't sure what he thought he was going to do if I did have a concussion, but it was still sweet of him to worry about me. He texted me again once he got home to make sure I was okay, and I promised that I would let him know when I woke up and how I was feeling.

Chapter Fifteen

I woke the next morning feeling fine, better than fine even. I reached for my phone to let Dylan know I was okay and saw that he'd obviously woken up before me.

Dylan: Morning babe, how are you feeling today? Any dizziness or nausea? X

I smirked. It felt good that he was thinking about me and wanting to know that I was okay.

Eren: Good morning, I'm fine, thank you. No

concussion here. Thanks for last night, I had a great time! X

He was obviously waiting for my text because he replied immediately.

Dylan: Glad you're okay and enjoyed last night. Does that mean there's going to be a second date? X

Someone better versed in dating than me might say that I should've let that question simmer and not show my interest so quickly. But I decided that would be too mean. Besides, I was too excited at the prospect of a second date to hold my answer in.

Eren: I would love a second date, if you want to? X

Dylan: Babe, I'm hoping for more than just two. X

I was giddy, practically bouncing up and down in bed. Iggy was excited, too, but only because I was. I grinned like an idiot and got out of bed, knowing Iggy would need to be let out. After I'd gone through my morning routine and sat down on Edward's chair with a brew, I thought of my twin and wondered what he would think of Dylan. They were very different people but I thought that they would've gotten along well, had they met. Edward had always been protective of me but thinking back to how much of a gentleman Dylan had been last night, I knew he would approve of how I was being treated. I burrowed further into the fluffy cushions at the thought and accepted the warmth that they offered.

Chapter Sixteen

Dylan's morning messages became routine, and we spoke intermittently all day every day until our next date. We were both skipping out on yoga on Monday to go to the cinema. Flo had offered to take Iggy to yoga with her and walk him while we were gone, and I had gratefully accepted. The look she'd given me when she'd first seen me after my date with Dylan told me that she was supportive of us. I had initially been nervous because I valued Flo as a friend and I didn't want to make things complicated for her so I was beyond pleased to have her approval.

We decided we would meet at the yoga class. I would drop Iggy there and we would walk to the cinema so we could both have a drink after and not worry about driving. I had my emergency twenty pounds in my phone case in case I needed to get a taxi back home alone, and Flo had a key to let Iggy back in, which she assured me she would post back through the letterbox once she had locked up. I was prepared for anything and everything.

I was in skinny jeans and a jumper for this date, wanting something a tad comfier and warmer seeing as we were walking. I had my knee-high boots on and my hair was in a ponytail, the curls bouncing in a line down my spine. After I'd dropped off my pooch, I went outside and found Dylan waiting, leaning next to the door, one leg propped up on the wall behind him. He was effortlessly sexy. Feeling brave, I sidled up to him and pressed a kiss to his cheek before he'd had a chance to turn and face me.

"Hey you," I breathed. He gripped my hips and twisted towards me, catching my lips with his.

"Hey yourself,"

I smiled at him, willing my body not to betray me and show him just how good I felt in his arms. He dropped them and entwined his fingers with mine, setting off in the direction of the cinema. We had settled on a fantasy film that had come out a few weeks before and was coming to the end of its run, so the screen should, in theory, be fairly quiet. There was nothing worse than going to see a film on opening night and it being packed—everyone whispering to each other, snack packets rustling, bottles being opened. Squished in like sardines because all the seats were full, I usually ended up with neither of my chair arms and a tall person in front of me. We had made the right choice because there were only three other people at the showing: one guy on his own and another couple.

We bought drinks and snacks, and I insisted again that we split the bill. Cinema food wasn't a joke. It was extortionate and there was no way I was letting him pay for all of that. We settled in our seats at the back and waited for the film to start. During the trailers, Dylan put his arm around my shoulders and as the film began, I settled into the seat and snuggled into his side. Eventually, he lifted the arm of the chair, removing the barrier between us, and I tucked myself into him. I snuck a peek at him and caught him looking down at me, the corners of his lips tilted ever so slightly upward. I stuck my tongue out at him and felt his body shudder with silent laughter. I didn't know why I did it but I was glad it amused him.

We watched the film wrapped up in each other and ate our snacks with no interruptions, until I heard the tiniest moan from the other side of the room. I lifted my head from Dylan's shoulder and tentatively looked around. The other couple were going at it, right there in the cinema. I held in my laughter and poked Dylan gently in the ribs. He jumped at my touch and looked down at me. I pointed discreetly towards the other couple and saw his eyes all but pop out of his head as he realised what was happening. I had to hand it to them, they were inconspicuous, but once you'd clocked what they were doing there was no doubting what you were looking at.

I had managed to keep my shock quiet. Dylan, however, let out an audible, "Jesus Christ", which in turn made me snort with laughter. The guy on his own turned to look at us then followed Dylan's eyeline and spotted the other two cinema goers, letting out a laugh as he realised their situation. The woman finally realised that they had been caught and there was a lot of fumbling before she finally ran out of the room, crossing in front of the screen, with the guy she was with hot on her heels. The three of us roared with laughter, so hard that it made my stomach hurt.

After a minute, a member of staff came in and asked if everything was okay. I couldn't answer, knowing I would burst out into another fit of giggles if I did. The guy on his own was closest to the attendant so he explained what had happened and the worker asked if we would mind leaving and being refunded for our tickets so they could clean. Of course we were fine and left the cinema laughing about the whole thing.

Dylan took me to a nearby pub that was quiet and cosy. A log fire dominated one side of the room and we took a table beside it. Dylan called the bar staff by name and I asked if he was a regular.

"No," he told me. "I worked here for a couple of months last year. I um... I got laid off from my job and needed money," he said, without quite meeting my eyes. I wondered why he'd brought me here if it made him uncomfortable.

I tilted my head to one side as our drinks were brought over. "Why are you acting weird about it?"

"Well, you've got this fancy job and I'm just an ex bartender." He shrugged.

"Hey!" I gave his shin a tap under the table. "I was a bartender once, too. You could still be a bartender for all I care. I loved my bar job," I told him, smiling wistfully.

"Well, obviously I'm out of bar work now," he

reminded me, his eyes regaining some of their sparkle. "But, I'm glad it doesn't bother you."

"It's nothing to be bothered by. A job's a job. Just because my job is in an office doesn't mean it's better." I took a sip of my gin and another thought occurred to me. "Did you really think I was stuck up like that?" His face dropped again and he grabbed my hand across the table as he scrambled to reassure me.

"Of course not. It's just, the last time I told a girl that, she looked down her nose at me like it was disgusting." He kept his grip on my hand, his gaze demanding my attention. "I brought you here because I *didn't* think you'd be like that. It's just something I'm personally a bit insecure about."

I squeezed his hand, nodded and smiled, showing him that I understood. His face relaxed and he sat back in his seat, looking relieved that the conversation was over.

"So, I wonder how the film ends," I mused, eyeing him over my wine glass.

A glint of mischief shone in his eyes as he replied, "Fuck that. I wonder what happened after they left. I'm not voyeuristic or anything but I'm dying to know how much she screamed at him." He laughed and I noticed how his eyes crinkled at the corners. I loved that he had laughter lines. It softened his features and gave the impression that he was usually cheerful. I needed that in my life. I was tired of constant sadness.

We stayed for a few drinks and I was teetering on the edge of tipsy by the time we set off home. We were going to get a taxi but the night wasn't as cold as we'd expected so we decided to walk. As it turned out, Dylan didn't live that far away from me—a ten minute walk at most. Even if he hadn't, he was the kind of guy who would have insisted on walking me to my door anyway. I spent the walk home with his jacket draped over my shoulders and my body tucked into his side.

We talked about favourites on the way home, taking it in turns to ask for one. I learnt that his favourite flavour of ice cream was chocolate, his favourite film was *Reservoir Dogs*, and his favourite band was Blue Oyster Cult. When we reached my door, I turned to him to say goodbye. I pressed my lips to his and parted them gently. He responded immediately, pressing me up against the door and wrapping his thick arms around my waist. When we came up for air his gaze was ferocious.

"I'm not ready to let you go yet," he whispered, dragging his nose along my cheek bone, dusting my face with his lips as he spoke.

"Well, in that case"—I pushed him away and put the key into the lock—"you should probably come in."

Flo must have had Iggy out walking for a while because his greeting was much shorter than usual before he took himself back to Edward's arm chair and promptly curled up to sleep. Suddenly nervous, I went to the kitchen, pulled out two wine glasses and the bottle he had brought when he came to dinner. Dylan followed me into the kitchen and saw my hands trembling as I poured us each a glass. He took the bottle from my hand and spun me around to look at him.

"What's wrong?"

"Nothing, I'm just nervous," I told him. I started picking at my fingernails, an obvious outward sign of my anxiety.

"Why?"

"Well, it's been a while, and I really like you and I don't want to mess this up," I said honestly, staring at our feet.

"Look at me, babe." He nudged my chin up with his finger. "First of all, I'm crazy about you. I highly doubt you're going to do anything that'll change that. Secondly, we're just having a drink. I'm not here expecting anything from you." The sincerity in his voice was mirrored in his gaze and I relaxed into his embrace. I felt his cheek rest on the top of my head and his breath ruffled my hair.

I eventually moved and asked him to finish pouring our drinks while I went to lock the front door and check my appearance in the hallway mirror. I wouldn't say that I had decided Dylan was staying the night, but locking the door whenever I was home at night was something I had always done, even before I lived alone. When I came back in, Dylan was standing in my living room, holding both glasses and looking at the photos on the mantelpiece. I internally cringed, knowing that the pictures there weren't particularly flattering. There were two photos of Edward and I, one as kids and one as adults, a photo of my parents, and most recently added, a photo of Iggy sitting on Edward's chair with a yellow bow tie on. I knew when Dylan had reached the picture of Iggy because he chuckled to himself and glanced at the fluff ball on the couch.

I came up next to him and took one of the glasses from his hand. "Wanna sit?" I pulled him to the sofa and we sat together. I leant into his side and tucked my feet up underneath me.

We sat in silence for a few minutes before Dylan piped up, "What's your favourite room in your house?" I laughed because it seemed so random but I was happy to continue our conversation from the walk home.

"The bathroom. If I could live in a hot bath, I would," I told him. "What about you?"

"My living room. My couch is insanely comfortable," he told me.

"I'll have to come and try it out sometime."

"Bring Iggy, too," he said, tilting his head towards the dog. "He seems like a man who loves a good cushion."

"He absolutely is and he will gladly accept the invitation." I laughed.

We talked and talked, the wine glasses forgotten on the coffee table, somehow moving ourselves closer and closer to each other until our noses were touching. I lost myself in his eyes and my hands absentmindedly moved up his chest, feeling the contours of his body. His hands had made their way to my waist but I still didn't feel close enough. I stood from the couch and pulled him with me, moving towards the stairs with the intention of taking things to the bedroom. Dylan pulled me to a stop as I climbed the first step, remembering my hesitancy earlier.

"Are you sure?" I leaned into him, now matching his height, and pressed my lips to his. I moved my hands up from his chest to his hair and nibbled on his bottom lip.

"I'm sure," I assured him. With that confirmation,

he lifted me up, my legs wrapped tightly around him and he climbed the stairs effortlessly, as if I were weightless.

I directed him to my bedroom, my lips grazing the shell of his ear and I took great pleasure in feeling his shiver each time. When we finally made it to my bedroom, rather than dropping me on the bed, he kept walking to the far wall and pressed me up against it, my legs still clamped around him. His fingers knotted in my hair as he covered my neck in kisses and nips, licking the spots he'd bitten to soothe my delicate skin.

I was so lost in how he made me feel that all I could do was moan and let him carry on as he pleased. Eventually, the feeling between my legs became too much and I found myself squirming against him, desperate for some friction to relieve the ache. He chuckled against my throat and spun us around before he let me down, holding me close so that I rubbed all the way down his body. He tucked a strand of hair behind my ear.

"You're so sexy, all hot and bothered like this." He kept a hand on my neck but made no further move, letting me take the lead on where things went from there. I gripped the front of his shirt and walked backwards until my legs hit the bed and I laid down, pulling him on top of me. He propped himself up on his forearms. I could feel him pressed on me without actually taking any of his weight, and his biceps popped out with the strain. I slid my hands under his top and dragged my fingers down his abs, feeling them flex under my touch. I tugged at the fabric covering his top half and moved to slide it up. He reached one arm over his head and pulled the top off, tossing it into the corner without taking his eyes off me. He cocked his head to one side and his mouth quivered into a cheeky grin.

"Better?"

"*Much* better, thanks," I told him, dragging a finger up his spine, and gently dragging my nails back down. He shivered as I did and buried his face into my collarbone.

"Jesus, Eren, what are you doing to me?" he growled, before licking up my neck.

Chapter Seventeen

I re-adjusted so that we were the right way up on the bed. I was glad I'd taken off my shoes downstairs because I wouldn't have wanted to stop what was happening to do it. I nudged at Dylan's shoes with my feet and he kicked them off without having to take any of his attention off me. I loved the feeling of him on top of me, and I was more than happy to run my hands all over his sculpted torso, but I could tell that he wasn't going to move things any further if I didn't give him more of a hint of what I wanted.

My legs were spread so that he was cradled between my thighs. I took advantage of that and bucked my hips, flipping us so that he was on his back. I sat up straight on top of him and pulled my shirt over my head, throwing it into the same corner as his. He ran his hands up my sides and I could feel the calluses on his palms from his work. The rough parts made me shiver and I gave a soft sigh when he reached my bra. His thumbs teased just beneath it and I pushed my chest out, seeking more of his touch. I reached behind my back and unclipped it, leaving my breasts free, my nipples peaked with a combination of arousal and the exposure to the cool air. I expected to feel his hands there immediately but instead he stared up at me, his eyes sparkling.

"Fuck, Eren, you look like you were made to be on top of me." The intensity of his words surprised me but I knew what he meant because he had looked the same way when he'd had me pressed against the wall.

I could see insecurity clouding his features when I didn't respond so I leant down, pressing my chest to his and whispered, "Maybe I was."

I woke up the next morning with my legs tangled in the bedding. I rolled over and reached out for Dylan but the spot where he had laid was empty. I felt my stomach dip as I realised that he must have left. Upset, I sat up looking for Iggy. He wasn't in the bedroom either so I put on my dressing gown and went downstairs to look for him. I did a double take when I saw him in the garden playing fetch with Dylan. I found my slippers at the back door and went out to join them.

Dylan had his back to me but Iggy spotted me and charged at me like a little cannon ball. I bent down to fuss with him and he set off again, doing excited laps around the lawn. I stood up straight, and tightened my dressing gown. I mumbled a good morning but avoided Dylan's eyeline, ashamed that I'd immediately jumped to the conclusion that he'd just upped and dashed on me. He took it the wrong way though and turned towards me, leaving a respectful distance between us.

"Eren, what's wrong?"

"Nothing," I muttered, shaking my head.

"Shit, you're not regretting last night, are you?" He turned around and ran his hands through his hair.

"No." I went to move in front of him and pulled his hands into mine. "I don't regret anything," I assured him, but he didn't look convinced and I knew I had to explain myself. "I was just embarrassed because, well, when I woke up and you weren't there, I thought you'd just gone." I watched as his face changed from worry, to relief, to contentment and suddenly I was in his arms.

"Not a chance, babe. Iggy was just whining, that's all. I didn't want him to wake you up," he promised. "I also didn't want to be naked in your garden and upset your neighbours so I thought I'd better get dressed."

We stayed there for a few minutes, wrapped up in each other, until my teeth started chattering and Dylan all but pushed me back into the house and insisted I put on something warmer. When I came back downstairs, Iggy had been fed and there was a coffee waiting for me on the kitchen side.

"Oh..." I was surprised. "You didn't need to do that," I said, wafting my hand in Iggy's general direction.

"I know. I just thought it might be helpful, save you a job." He shrugged sheepishly and I felt immediately guilty. Why couldn't I just say thank you?

Wanting to rectify the situation and put our morning back on track, I hopped up and sat myself on the table so that he was in front of me. I pulled him into a hug and ran my fingers through his silky hair.

"Thank you. You've made my morning easier," I

told him before letting my arms drop and reaching for my coffee.

"Anytime, babe. Consider my morning services reserved for you." He winked and pressed a kiss to my forehead.

Feeling like I should repay the favour, I made bacon sandwiches, which caused Iggy to shoot us dirty looks as we ate. I'd slept in later than usual and by the time we'd washed up after breakfast it was already eleven o'clock. I had no plans but I didn't want Dylan to feel like he *had* to stay so I tried to slyly find out what he was planning on doing.

"What are you up to today?"

"No plans, what about you? Do you need me to go?"

"God no, I was just wondering. We could do something, if you want?" I suggested, hoping he would agree.

"Sure babe, I just need to nip home for a shower and to change. You could come with me though, try out my famously comfy sofa while you wait?"

I ummed and aahed about going to Dylan's house for the day. I didn't want to intrude on his personal space, but I also didn't want to end our time together before I had to. Dylan had said that he was more than happy for Iggy to come with us, and I had a few toys and some doggy bags in my handbag. I was running out of excuses rapidly, and I didn't even really know why I was making them anyway. I dragged out my shower for as long as I could and came downstairs dressed and ready to go. Before I'd gone upstairs, Iggy had been demanding Dylan's attention by lying belly up on the couch next to him, nudging him repeatedly with his little snout. When I came back, he was sitting in Dylan's lap with his front paws on his chest, trying to chew on his chin. Dogs were weird.

We walked to Dylan's house hand in hand. I tried to leave my anxiety at home so we could enjoy our time together, and we detoured through the park so that Iggy could have another run around. Once at his house, Dylan disappeared for a quick shower and change, leaving me in his surprisingly cosy living room. Edward had always left me in charge of decoration at home and his room had always been ridiculously basic. I expected a house that only a man lived in would be just as minimalistic, but Dylan's style was much closer to mine. There was a blanket slung over the back of the sofa, a log burner in the fireplace and a thick rug in front of it.

Iggy made himself at home immediately so I followed suit and sank into the couch cushions. Dylan was right; it was insanely comfortable. The log burner was on, keeping me nice and toasty, and I felt my eyelids drooping despite myself. It had been a late one last night and I had recently become more accustomed to an afternoon nap.

I felt something moving down by my feet and I shuffled around, trying to move away from the source of the discomfort. I rolled and my hand hit something. The sound that came after told me that what I'd actually hit was someone. I rubbed my eyes and sat up in a daze, trying to figure out what had been a dream and what was actually happening.

"Morning, sleepyhead," I heard from the floor just in front of me. "You okay?"

"Why are you on the floor?" I croaked, my voice thick with sleep.

"I didn't want to wake you up by sitting on the sofa," he explained. He moved up onto his knees and faced me. "Would you like a brew?"

"Please." I nodded. He leaned in towards me and I clamped my lips shut, certain I must have morning breath, or I guess, afternoon breath. But when he was close enough to kiss, I forgot to care and pulled him into me.

We spent the rest of the afternoon on the sofa, curled up together under a blanket while Iggy luxuriated on the rug in front of the fireplace. We were content just being with each other and watching a cheesy romcom until my stomach ruined the ambience by growling to remind me that I hadn't eaten since breakfast.

"Shit, I should go. I need to make tea," I told Dylan, sitting forward to get off the couch. I looked at him and he seemed taken aback. "What?"

"I have a kitchen, with food in it," he hinted, raising his eyebrows. "I could make you something to eat,"

"I don't want to inconvenience you, though."

"You're not. I need to eat, too, you know?" He smiled, shaking his head at me. He took my hand and pulled me off the couch. "Let's go and see what I have in the fridge."

We decided to make stir fry. Dylan said he didn't need help but it felt wrong to just sit and let him cook for me so I hovered around the kitchen, chopping and peeling and stirring—basically, doing anything I possibly could without getting in the way. It was nice to see him in his element. He drifted around the kitchen, barely looking at what he was doing but somehow still managing. It was like he was in tune with everything around him, myself included. He conveniently manoeuvred around me and we worked together in tandem.

I set out a bowl of unseasoned chicken for Iggy and we sat down on the floor to eat, picnic style. I couldn't stop that guttural moan that came out when I tasted that first bite. Fuck me, the man could cook. He smirked as I devoured the meal and I noted how his chest seemed to inflate with pride.

"That good?" he asked

"So good I might take yours," I warned him with a grin. "You better eat fast."

We carried on slurping our noodles in comfortable silence, which was weird for me because I'd always felt like I needed background noise. It was different around Dylan; the anxiety didn't creep in like it normally would have. When we were done, we stayed on the floor, wanting to be cosy around the fire. The weather had turned and rain was coming down in buckets, pounding against the windows. I reclined back into Dylan's arms and closed my eyes, letting myself feel content in my surroundings. My head rose and fell with his chest, and the rhythm of that combined with his fingers running up and down my arm were enough to make me never want to move again. I couldn't believe how comfortable I felt with him and in that moment, I allowed myself to enjoy it.

Despite me trying to tell him I could walk, Dylan insisted on giving me a lift home.

"I know it's not far away, but it's pissing it down, Eren. Just let me drive you," he argued. I eventually agreed and I was secretly glad I had because if I'd walked, I would've been soaked to the bone and Iggy would've probably had to swim rather than walk. I said goodbye to Dylan in the car, not wanting him to get any wetter than he had to, and hurried inside, feeling freezing within seconds so I went straight to the bathroom to run the hottest bath of my life. As I stepped into the bathtub, my phone pinged with a message from Dylan.

Dylan: I loved spending the day with you. X

He was so sweet to be messaging me already. It had only been about ten minutes since he'd dropped me off.

Eren: I had the best time. Thanks again for the lift home! X

I put my phone on the sink so I could recline in the hot water. I was so cold that my toes and fingers started to feel prickly when they were submerged. Iggy wandered into the bathroom to see what was happening and walked right back out again when he realised how humid it was in there. When I lifted my arm out of the water, steam was rising off it. The windows and mirror were all fogged up and I was loving every minute of it. I began to think about Dylan and how the past two days had been. I had loved our time together and he was a complete sweetheart, but I was worried. I didn't want to rush into something serious and lose the independence I had only recently gotten a handle on. I knew that I was going to have to handle this delicately, otherwise I would end up pushing him away and ruining what we had. I reached for my phone and there was another text.

Dylan: You're welcome. I would've felt awful if you'd walked and ended up with a cold. X

Eren: You're so sweet. Don't worry about me. I'm in a nice hot bubble bath away from the rain. X

Dylan: Damn, I wish I'd come in to see that ;) X

Eren: Trust me, bathtime Eren is not attractive. I have a messy bun and a face mask. I look like a swamp creature! X

Dylan: A hot swamp creature. X

I had to laugh; I'd never been called a hot swamp creature before. In fact, I wasn't sure anyone had ever been called that before. I put my phone down again and relaxed back against the edge of the tub. I could see just how quickly I was falling for Dylan and it was a mad mix of scary and exciting.

We spent the next couple of weeks going on dates, having hot sex and spending entire weekends together. We were so compatible and had so much fun together that I was scared to make any changes in case I ruined it.

Chapter Eighteen

We had texted every day and spent hours on the phone to each other, but I didn't actually see Dylan that week until yoga on Thursday. Flo had told me before we started that she was free on Saturday so we'd arranged for me to go to her house to talk about the branding I'd come up with and what we were going to do from there. Dylan had offered to give me a lift but I'd declined and told him I was working overtime so I would be coming straight from the office. He seemed fine with it but I still felt bad. It's not like I was lying. I was going into the office because I had a lunchtime meeting and then I needed to be able to print out mock ups and what not, but I suppose I could've rearranged my day if I'd wanted to. But it would have meant getting to the office earlier and I wanted my lie in dammit!

We agreed that Dylan would come over on Friday after we'd both finished work and that we would get a takeaway. With all the yoga I'd been doing I felt like I could justify some junk food.

Angela knew I'd been spending time with Dylan and she mercilessly teased me all of Friday for being so eager to get home and see him. He had been texting me all day, telling me how much he'd missed me, that he was dying to see me again, that he couldn't wait to have me all to himself for the night. His messages made me deliriously happy, and the moment five o'clock rolled around, I bolted for the door and drove home without a second thought.

I walked Iggy and then jumped into the shower quickly before getting dressed in some lounge pants and a vest top. I wanted to look good but also like I wasn't trying too hard. I pulled my hair into two braids and did a quick tidy of the living room. I was just putting the hoover away when I heard Dylan knock on the door. I shouted for him to come in and heard Iggy clattering about to greet him.

"I'm in the kitchen," I yelled, trying to force the hoover back into the pantry.

"Want a hand?" Dylan asked behind me after seeing me fight the blasted thing.

"Nah, fuck it. Let it stay out in the corner and think about what it's done." I glared at it scathingly before turning to Dylan and bouncing over to him. I took him by surprise and rolled onto my tiptoes to give him a kiss. He returned my advances and I could feel the smile on his lips. I nipped teasingly at his bottom lip and ran my tongue along it to soothe the sting I was sure I'd left behind. "How was your day, my love?"

"Pretty average, I think my evening's going to overshadow it," he said, pulling me closer for a hug.

I rested my head on his collar bone and let out a contented sigh. "I've missed you," I told him.

"I've missed you too."

We ordered a curry and I placed an online order so I could pay by card without telling Dylan. I hoped he wouldn't ask about it but of course, I wasn't that lucky. He went to grab his wallet when the door went and I had to tell him it wasn't necessary.

"Why not? Let me get this one," he urged.
"There's really no need. I already paid by card when I

ordered," I told him. He made a face but I told him that he could pay next time, and he seemed happier.

We both ate far too much, and by the time we were done I was incredibly grateful that my lounge pants had an elastic waistband. We lay together on the couch and turned on the television. Dylan tried to wash up but I told him I would sort it tomorrow and that I just wanted to relax with him. We spooned on the sofa. One of his arms was under my head, the other around my waist, holding me against him. Our bodies fit together like a jigsaw puzzle and I snuggled as close to him as I could. I heard his breathing slow down and I realised that he'd fallen asleep behind me. I didn't move for a long time, not wanting to wake him up. I knew that his job was very physically demanding and I wanted him to get as much rest as possible.

I had to move eventually so I could let Iggy out before bed, and when I came back, Dylan was still dead to the world. I shook his shoulder to wake him and he stumbled upstairs with me, got undressed and into bed, barely opening his eyes. He was flat out again as soon as his head hit the pillow. I lay beside him, taking advantage of him being asleep to really look at him. I stared at his dark lashes, so long and full that it felt wildly unfair that they'd been given to a man. His stubble was filling out and getting closer to beard territory but it suited him and made him look more rough and ready than if he had been clean shaven. I could've spent hours reviewing the length of his nose, the definition of his cheek bones and the shape of his strong jaw, but I could feel myself slipping away into sleep, and eventually I let my eyes close, still facing him.

My alarm went off at ten o'clock, waking us both. I rolled over to hit the snooze button with a groan and as I did so, Dylan's hands landed on me and pulled me into his side. I rested my head on his chest and threw an arm over his stomach, using the extra ten minutes in bed to enjoy the feeling of being wrapped up in him rather than sleeping.

"Do you have to go to work?" he grumbled into my hair, making me laugh.

"Unfortunately, I do, otherwise I can't pay bills,"

"Just come and live with me. It'll be fine." I laughed again but said nothing. His thumb rubbed up and down the dip at my waist and he fiddled with the hem of my top. "Why are you wearing pyjamas?"

"What else would I wear to bed?"

"Nothing," he suggested. I could feel his eyes on me and guessed that he was picturing it.

"Don't laugh when I explain," I warned him, knowing he would regardless. "There are two reasons why I don't usually sleep naked. Firstly, if there's a fire and the firefighters have to drag me out of the house, I don't want to be on the street naked in front of my neighbours. Secondly, I'm scared that a spider might crawl up my vagina."

He tried to hold it in but I could feel his entire body convulsing as he silently howled at my answer. "What the fuck Eren?" he choked out eventually.

"Look, I know the spider thing is irrational and would never happen but it freaks me out." I buried my head in his chest, embarrassed. I knew exactly how ridiculous it was but after I'd learnt that people ate spiders in their sleep, I'd wondered where else they might end up and I'd scared myself.

"You slept naked the first time I was here, though," he reminded me.

"Well, yeah, but I fell asleep still naked so I couldn't help it." I shrugged. "If I'd stayed awake after the sex, I would have put pants on." He was still laughing and I ended up giggling too. All the noise woke Iggy and we ended up getting out of bed before the alarm went off a second time to let him out.

I went for a quick shower and got ready for my meeting, and Dylan brought me a mug of tea and some toast. When I was ready to go, he swept me into a hug and pressed an intense kiss to my lips.

"Go and kill that meeting, baby," he whispered in my ear. "I'll see you later."

Chapter Nineteen

I'd have loved to say that the meeting went well, but overall it just went weirdly. I definitely should have just stayed in bed with my man. The meeting was with a long-term client who I had worked with a couple of times over the last few years. We had gotten to know each other on a more personal level over time, but it had been over six months since we'd last spoken.

He started the meeting by asking how Edward was and I told him in a very shaky voice that he had unfortunately passed away. The client was mortified and apologised profusely. I told him not to worry because there was no way he could have known but the tone of the meeting was weird from there onwards.

I spent the whole time trying not to burst into tears and he barely said a word other than to say he liked what I'd come up with and that, once again, he was very sorry. I was relieved when the online meeting was over and I gave myself some time to just cry at my desk.

Iggy had been such a good boy on the sofa during my meeting but when he heard me begin to sob, he came straight over and pawed at my leg until I picked him up. I'd brought some make up and extra clothes with me, so once I'd calmed down and done all the printing I needed to do, I went to change and to sort out my make-up in the bathroom mirror.

I had cried a lot of my makeup away so I raided Angela's emergency face wipe stash and just started again from the beginning. By the time I was ready to set off to Flo's house, it was six o'clock and I was very much in danger of being late. When I'd planned my day out, I hadn't accounted for time spent crying so I had to skip nipping to the shop for a bottle of wine and hoped like hell that my work would make up for my bad manners.

Dylan came to answer the door when I finally arrived and when he took in my face, he knew something was different. "You didn't look like this when you left this morning, did you?"

"No, I had to re-do my make-up. Let me say hi to Flo and I'll explain." I went to greet my hostess and she sent me to the living room with a glass of wine to relax while she finished cooking.

I dropped down onto the couch next to Dylan and rested my head on his shoulder, exhausted with the day. He wrapped an arm around my shoulder and squeezed me into him. "So, what happened?"

"I cried and messed up my make-up at work so I had to take it all off and start again," I explained with a sigh.

"Why, what happened?" he asked, twisting to see me better. I could hear the alarm in his voice and I quickly explained my conversation with the client. "Eren, babe, why didn't you ring me?"

"Why would I? You couldn't have fixed it and it would have just interrupted your day."

"I'm your boyfriend. You're allowed to interrupt my day!"

I opened my mouth and snapped it closed again, forgetting what I was originally going to say. "You're my boyfriend?" I asked. We hadn't talked about labelling what was happening between us and I didn't really know where I stood with him.

"Well, I thought so. We've been doing a lot of boyfriend girlfriend things. Dates, sex, sleepovers. I've been thinking of you as my girlfriend," he admitted. "Should I not?" he asked, his voice wavering a little.

I looked at him with a watery smile. "I didn't realise you looked at us that way. It makes me happy that you do, though," I told him honestly.

"So, it's agreed, we're a couple. So that means you tell me when things like this happen so I can comfort you, okay?" His hands had moved to cup my face and he was staring deep into my eyes as he said the words. I could see that he really meant it and I considered myself the luckiest girl in the world.

"Agreed," I breathed before his lips crushed mine. I kissed him back fiercely, the fingers on my free hand spiking into his hair before a clatter from the kitchen reminded us that we were in his sister's house and we broke apart with a nervous giggle on my part.

Chapter Twenty

"Eren, these are incredible," Flo gushed when I showed her my ideas. We had settled on my design with the willow tree behind the word *Flow* and a stream of water beneath reflecting it all. The colours were all watery and soft and it felt calm and inviting.

I was proud of what I'd managed to create, and seeing Flo's reaction made all my work feel worthwhile. The logo matched her whimsical demeanour and worked well with the meditative side of yoga. I showed her the mock up business cards and flyers I'd made as well as the social media graphics, and by the end of everything she was beaming. Her warm smile lit up the room and I basked in it after my somewhat bumpy day.

Dylan was quiet the whole time and it made me self conscious to think that maybe he didn't like what I'd done. It shouldn't have mattered because it was his sister's business, not his, but I wanted his approval. I hated the part of me that craved his praise but there was no denying it was there. I excused myself to let Iggy outside and tried to talk some sense into myself. I was emotional; it had been a long day and I was probably reading too much into things.

I steeled myself to go back inside but as I opened the door, Dylan was directly in front of me. Iggy ran right into the hallway, weaving around us but we stayed put. He was just staring at me and I couldn't read the feelings that passed through his eyes. I was apprehensive and I went to speak but didn't get a chance. He pulled me into a hug so tight and swift that it knocked the air out of me. I had no idea what was going on but I relaxed in his hold anyway. He didn't pull back to look at me but his stubble grazed my cheek and I heard his gruff voice in my ear.

"You're so talented, babe. What you've done in there has just blown my mind."

"Really?" I asked, still unsure of myself.

"Really. I had no idea what to say when I saw it because I was just in complete awe of you,"

I felt so much better knowing that he liked my work that I got myself a little choked up. My designs were something I'd always worked hard on and Edward had always given me so much encouragement that I'd felt deflated about it since we'd lost him. I felt that I would never be as good without him to push me along. I was so relieved to know that I still had it and that there was still someone out there who would support me.

We went back inside and had a few more drinks with Flo after she'd let me know how many items she wanted. I felt good about what I'd done for her and was glad I had some way to show my gratitude for how much her classes had helped me.

When it came time to leave, I knew that I'd had too much to drink to drive so I told Dylan I was going to walk but that he could stay there.

He frowned at me. "Don't be ridiculous. I'm not having you walk home alone at this time of night! Anything could happen to you."

I started to protest but Flo interjected. "He's right.

It's nearly midnight and it's pitch black."

"Besides," Dylan purred in my ear, "I was kind of hoping we could spend the rest of the night together anyway." I shivered as his breath tickled me and I nodded, squeezing his hand.

The walk home was uneventful and I definitely could have done it alone. But I was glad I didn't, especially when Dylan pulled me into his side and began detailing everything he wanted to do to me when we got home. He had a very dirty mind that he'd been keeping from me, and his words very much matched it. If we hadn't had Iggy with us, there's a very good chance I would've dragged him somewhere quiet and shadowy before we got back to the house.

When we got home, Dylan made good on his promises. As soon as I locked the door behind us, he was at my back, pressing me up to the wood so I couldn't turn around. He ran his hands up my stomach, my chest, my neck—he swept my hair to one side so he could lick and suck his way up the sensitive skin there. One hand went up my top and the other to my waist, unbuttoning my jeans and skimming the edge of my lace panties. He teased me mercilessly, touching me over my underwear but never dipping underneath. I moaned at his touch, unable to help myself, and he responded by grinding his pelvis against my backside. I could feel just how turned on he was and I wiggled against him, hoping to do some teasing of my own.

"Dylan please," I panted, knowing I was a mess.

"Tell me what you need babe," he encouraged, his teeth grazing my ear.

"You, always you."

He growled from behind me and pulled me away from the door, kissed me until I went dizzy and swept me off my feet, not putting me down until we reached my bed.

When I woke up, I was sore. My muscles were aching in places they'd never ached before. Dylan had treated me with attention that bordered on worship the previous night, and I'd made every effort to give as good as I'd got. He was still asleep beside me but I could hear Iggy whining at the door, so I slipped out of his arms and went downstairs to let him out. I made a brew then sat in Edward's chair and enjoyed the peace that was exclusive to a Sunday morning. I heard Dylan coming down the stairs before I saw him and turned my head in his direction.

"Morning. Do you want a brew?"

"I'd love one." He grinned, coming to kiss me. "But don't get up. I'll do it myself." By the time he finished his sentence, I was already standing with my mug in my hand.

"Don't worry, I want another one anyway."

Dylan shook his head slightly but with an affectionate smile on his face. I ignored him and went to fill the kettle. Dylan pulled out a mug and went to the fridge for the milk.

"What are you doing? I said I'd sort it."

"I'm helping," he told me simply. "I don't want you waiting on me," he teased before bending down to grab the stuffed toy Iggy had dropped at his feet.

After our brew, we decided to go out for breakfast. No one wanted to cook on a Sunday and we were no exception to that rule. We stopped by Dylan's so he could shower and get changed, and he joked that he might need to move some clothes to my house for times like these.

"Yeah, just move in, why don't you?" I snorted. His face changed. It was barely perceptible but I saw a flash of *something*. He didn't bring up whatever he was feeling, so I didn't either, thinking it best to let him tell me in his own time. We talked about our plans for the week. Dylan was ridiculously busy all week, to the point that he would be skipping yoga classes. I was sad that I wouldn't have any time with him but I tried to hide it as best I could. I had things to do anyway—work was busy and I hadn't spent much time with my parents or Layla recently, so I decided to make use of my week to rectify that. Dylan kept looking at me throughout the day with a confused expression, like he was trying to figure something out. Whenever I asked, he said it was nothing.

As the day wore on, Dylan got quieter. I tried to overcompensate, chatting nonsense about things neither of us really cared about until he had to leave. It did no good and eventually we ended the night sitting in silence watching the telly. I locked up and went to bed with a knot in my chest. I had no idea what was going on but I didn't think it was good.

Chapter Twenty-One

I skipped yoga on Monday, and worked late. Angela was working late too so it wasn't like I was lonely. Dylan had texted me in the morning but I didn't get a chance to reply until lunch. I'd put my phone down when I got into the office and had just forgotten to pick it up since. By the time I realised what I'd done, he had tried to ring me and had sent another message. I felt awful and I tried to call him back immediately but had to leave him a message.

We continued to miss each other's calls all day, and

it was eight o'clock in the evening before we actually spoke for the first time.

"Hey, baby, how was your day?"

"It was alright, busy. How about yours?" I asked

"It was fine, just tiring. We were missing two labourers today so we had to make up for it."

"That's shit. Maybe you should have an early night?" I suggested, lightly.

"Trying to get me off the phone already?" He let out a dry laugh.

"What? No, of course not. I just thought it might help!" I argued in defence of myself.

"Nah, I'm good. I'd rather talk to you for a bit longer. I've missed you today."

"I've missed you, too."

We stayed on the phone for two hours before Dylan finally admitted defeat and succumbed to sleep. I made a mental note to make more of an effort to text him regularly tomorrow. It was an honest accident and I didn't want to give him the impression that I didn't care.

Tuesday passed like Monday, but I did make more time to speak to Dylan and things felt better between us. I managed to get everything done through the rest of the week that I wanted to do, but on Saturday morning I was hit with something unexpected.

There was a knock on the door at ten o'clock that I wasn't expecting. I opened it to find my parents at the door, looking uncomfortable.

"What's up?" I asked, alarmed enough by their expressions to forgo a polite greeting.

They gave me tight smiles and looked at each other nervously. "Can we come in?" Dad asked.

"Erm yeah, sure," I said, stepping aside so they could enter.

I put the kettle on and we sat down in the living room. I was tense to say the least, and started picking at my cuticles while I waited for them to spit out whatever it was they'd come to say. Eventually, after some less than subtle nudges from my mum, Dad got to the point.

"Look, sweetheart, I know you haven't been in Edward's room since the accident but we need to go in and get all his personal documents out so we can start closing his accounts and whatnot now probate has come through."

I was shocked. I didn't even know they'd applied for probate. I glanced at the stairs and took a shaky breath. I knew I'd have to go in there eventually but I'd been avoiding it for months. I nodded, without saying a thing, and led the way up the stairs. We got to the door and I put my hand on the brass knob, willing myself to be able to twist it. Eventually, I felt my dad's big hand over my own and I let him turn it for me so we could go in.

It smelt musty in there. The pile of dirty laundry was still in the basket. There were clean clothes folded on his bed, waiting to be put away. His desk and bookshelf had a fine layer of dust over them. I felt horrendous. I never should have allowed this to happen. Edward would be ashamed if he knew how I'd shut this room off as if it didn't exist. As if *he* didn't exist. Seeing his dressing gown hanging on the back of the door was the last straw and I lost control of myself, dropped to the floor and broke down in tears.

I couldn't catch my breath, couldn't see through the tears, couldn't hear through the sound of my own heaving sobs. I could feel arms around me but it didn't help. I was lost in a pool of grief that I thought I'd managed to wade out of. My dad helped me leave the room, like I was an injured child, and gently guided me to my bedroom, where I crawled under the duvet and cried myself to sleep barely two hours after I'd woken up.

When I woke up again, my eyes were burning and my throat was raw. I went to splash cold water on my face and saw that my skin was blotchy and pink. I decided to get dressed and take Iggy for a walk, hoping that the fresh air would do me some good. There was a note on the fridge saying that my parents had found what it was they needed and had let themselves out. I took it down and binned it, not wanting to think about what had happened earlier.

I decided I'd drive to the beach and take Iggy for a walk there. I thought we could both do with a change of scenery. As we were leaving, Dylan's car pulled up. I wasn't expecting to see him until much later in the evening and I was torn on how I felt. I was happy to see him, of course, but I also felt like shit and knew that I looked even worse. He parked the car and jogged up to me, a smile on his face.

"Dylan, what are you doing here?" I asked, shocked.

"I finished early. I thought I'd surprise you," he said, pulling flowers out from behind his back. I took in the fact that he was here, that he'd brought me a bunch of yellow roses just because, and that, combined with the awful start to my day set me off bawling again.

Iggy started yapping as I embarrassed myself in the street, and Dylan pulled me and the dog back through my still open front door and released Iggy from his lead. He pulled me into his arms and let me soak the front of his shirt with my tears, the flowers forgotten on the floor. I tried so hard to stop the flow of my cries, but every time I came close, I'd remember something else about Edward that would set me off all over again. It took half an hour before I was able to stop the tears long enough to apologise for being such a mess. Dylan had tugged at my arms and sat me on the sofa while I was crying and left me in place to calm down whilst he made me a cup of tea. When he came back, he set the mugs on the table and sat down, and I leant my head in his lap. He started stroking my hair and I told him about my morning.

Chapter Twenty-Two

"Why didn't you ring me?" he asked, once I'd finished explaining.

"You couldn't have done anything, and I didn't want to worry you when you were busy at work," I started but I felt him shift beneath me. I sat up and watched him turn so he was facing me, and he looked so sad that my chest hurt.

"Eren, we've been through this. This is the kind of thing that you should come to me about. We're together. We're a couple. We're supposed to support and help each other."

"But this is stuff that comes from before I knew you," I mumbled.

"I don't care! I got into this relationship knowing that you'd been through this. I knew that you were going to have days like this and I want to be there to help get you through them. I can't do that if you refuse to tell me how you're feeling."

I didn't know what to say so I just sat as he surveyed me. He suddenly stood up and ran his hands through his hair.

"Look, I know it's early on but I feel a real connection with you and I am so completely smitten with you that it's scary." I swallowed, waiting for him to finish his thought. "But maybe..." He stopped.

"Maybe what?"

"Maybe, it isn't the same for you. You keep pushing me away, not telling me stuff, not letting me help you or take care of you. You won't even let me buy you dinner. Maybe you just aren't feeling what I'm feeling. I know this is awful timing because you've had a shit day and I don't want to put any pressure on you, but I feel like you need to know and then this way if you aren't interested you've got an out."

I stared open mouthed at him, unable to believe what I was hearing.

"No! That's not what this is." I jumped off the couch to go to him but he cringed back from me, and I felt it like a blow to the chest. "Dylan, please, just hear me out, okay?" He nodded but stayed where he was, looking deflated and miserable. "This isn't about me not being in the same place as you, okay? I am so, so borderline obsessed with you but I've only recently started to be completely independent, and I'm scared that if I let you in and forget how to live on my own, I might lose you and then I'll be back to square one again with no idea how to claw back to where I am now," I finished, staring up at him.

His eyes were glistening with unshed tears and I hated that I was the cause of them. All I wanted was to grab him and shake him, and make him see exactly how I felt but I couldn't. All I could do was explain as best I could and hope that he understood what I was trying to get through to him.

"I swear, it's not that I'm not invested in us because I am."

I couldn't take the distance between us any longer so I reached for him, gently taking his hand in mine. He didn't shake me off, which I took as a good sign, and I moved closer to him. He finally met my eyes and

I prayed to anyone that would listen that he saw how much I meant everything I said.

"Can I be completely honest?"

"Of course." I nodded eagerly, glad he was at least saying *something*.

"I know we haven't been together long and it sounds ridiculous, but I know that I love you. You are everything I've ever wanted in a partner and it's been killing me thinking that you might not be completely in this with me. I'm not expecting you to say it back. I know that it's too soon for most people, but I thought I better just put all my cards on the table so you know." His gaze moved from me to the hallway. "I understand if this is too much for you or if you need time or space," he finished, trying to pull his hand out of mine.

I tightened my grip on him, not wanting to let him go anywhere that was away from me.

"I can't say that right now," I whispered. "I wish I could but I just can't, not yet." He nodded again but still didn't look back at me. Even without eye contact, I could see that he was spiralling and the look of devastation on his face was agonising, "But that doesn't mean that I don't feel anything for you and it doesn't mean that I won't say it ever. I'm absolutely crazy about you and I don't want this —us— to end." I tugged on his hand, trying to get him to respond. "Babe, please say something."

He sniffed and rubbed at his jaw before he responded. "You mean that?" he asked. There was none of the confidence in his voice that I'd grown so accustomed to.

"Of course I do," I promised him, my eyes beseeching him to see how much he meant to me. He leant down and pressed his lips to mine and I kissed him back hungrily, trying to force my feelings into him, begging him to feel how much I needed him and wanted him. I put my all into my kiss and when we broke apart, I was terrified that it wasn't enough.

"I don't mind that you can't tell me you love me right now," he told me, his forehead pressed to mine. "As long as I know that you're in this as much as I am."

"Of course I am. I promise you I am."

I could see the dark cloud lifting off him. I wrapped my arms around his neck and he sagged into my hold. I wound my fingers into his hair and mumbled to him how much he meant to me and that I wasn't going anywhere.

When I woke up the next day, Dylan was still in bed next to me, his arm around my waist. It had been an emotional night of sex as I tried to show him everything that my fragile heart was too scared to put into words. I had never seen him so defeated as he'd looked the previous night, and the memory of it, knowing that I was the reason for it, made me wince. I never wanted to hurt him that way again. I worried about how long he would wait to hear those magic words from me. Eventually, I would lose him if I didn't show my commitment. I needed to do something to show him how I felt, even if I couldn't say the obvious thing. It wasn't as if I didn't *want* to say it but there was an irrational part of my brain telling me that if I told him I loved him, I'd lose him. I didn't know what to do, and I could feel my heart pounding as I considered the consequences of my own messed up mind. Edward would have known exactly what I should do.

I slid out of the bed as quietly as I could and tiptoed down the hall to Edward's bedroom. I put out a shaking hand and held onto the doorknob. I flicked my wrist and the door swung open. I steeled myself, knowing this would hurt. I stepped over the threshold and sat on the edge of the bed. Tears rolled down my cheeks and I made no effort to stop them or wipe them away. I looked around the room, taking note of everything that was there. His dressing gown hanging off the back of the door. His desk with his computer, his bookshelf with all of his old favourites on, many of which had become my favourites, too, thanks to Edward's enthusiasm for sharing the stories with me. The pile of dirty clothes was still in the washing basket and there was a jumper slung on the back of his computer chair. I got up and took it, pulling it over my head. He must have worn it not long before we'd left the house because it still smelt of him. Fresh tears welled in my eyes and I left the room, knowing I'd had enough for one day.

I went back to my room and Dylan was still asleep. I crawled back into bed and wriggled my way back into his arms. He stirred and his grip around me tightened. I sniffled and felt his lips press onto my forehead.

"You okay baby?"

"I went back into Edward's room but I got too upset so I came back for a cuddle," I explained, nestling further into his warmth.

"I'm sorry you got upset," he mumbled into my hair. "Do you want me to make you breakfast?"

"No, thank you. I just want to stay here for a while," I told him. His arms cinched around me, hauling me impossibly closer, and I drifted back to sleep right there in his embrace.

Dylan was still holding me when I woke up again. The television had been turned on and I'd moved in my sleep, now draped over him, one of his arms around my waist and the other stroking my hair. I sighed and stretched upwards to kiss his neck.

"Are you feeling better?"

"Much better," I told him, settling myself back down with my head on his chest.

"Good," he whispered, his fingers fiddling with the jumper I was wearing. "I'm guessing this came back from the room with you?" he asked gently.

"Yeah, I thought it might make me feel better." I shrugged.

"Did it work?"

"I think so. The jumper and you," I told him. I looked up and saw him smiling down at me. The traces of last night still lingered in his eyes but I knew I was on my way to fixing the damage I had done.

Chapter Twenty-Three

Eight months later

Dylan and I gradually became closer than ever. I had considered everything that had come out in our discussion and decided I needed to get myself some grief counselling. That, combined with Dylan's support, made me feel more confident and with his constant affection, I grew even more comfortable in our relationship. We were rarely apart, alternating our time between his home and mine. Iggy had things in both homes and was more than happy to have a regular change of scenery. Everything felt like it was falling into place.

Counselling was helping me immensely and I had seen a change within myself that made me happy and proud. It became easier to talk about Edward and I found myself enjoying sharing those parts of my life with Dylan. He would listen intently to my endless stories and asked questions about him. I had held all of this back, thinking that talking about my brother would make me miss him more but I found that not to be the case. The more stories I told, the closer I felt to the man I had lost, and the closer I felt to the one I had so recently gained. I spent much less time moping by myself and more time celebrating the good times we'd had together. I even took Dylan to Edward's grave, hoping it would help me connect the two somehow. I would have loved for the two of them to have met but this was the closest I was ever going to get so I sucked it up as best I could. I still had my off days, of course, but I really felt like I was moving in the right direction. We had learnt how to co-exist without being in each other's pockets, and I was getting closer and closer to being able to tell him what I knew was in my heart.

The day started like any other: we had breakfast together, said goodbye on the doorstop, and both headed off to work. Iggy was with me and I parked a few streets away from the office so he could have a walk before work. The weather was getting colder, bordering on icy. I was glad I was wearing trainers. I looked ridiculous combining them with my charcoal grey pinafore but I would've looked even more ridiculous if I was on my arse in the middle of the road because I'd slipped in my heels. Changing shoes at work was the obvious answer.

As always, Iggy pelted it up the stairs to Angela's desk for his routine morning treat, and as always, Angela was more than willing to oblige. I was so glad that she loved my little fluff ball as much as she did, especially then. I was about to start my lunch break when I heard Flo's voice at the front desk, higher pitched than usual and desperate.

"I need Eren. It's an emergency, please." Hearing those words, I was on my feet in seconds and hurried to Angela's desk.

"Flo, what is it?"

"Oh, thank God. Eren, I'm sorry it's Dylan. There's been an accident at work. They didn't say what it was but he's been blue-lighted to hospital and we need to go." I froze up, unable to process what she was saying to me. I gaped at her and looked at Angela for guidance.

"Give me your keys. I'll take care of Iggy and hold

the fort here," she instructed. "Don't worry about anything here, just go."

I went back to my office to grab my bag and passed Angela the keys on my way out. Flo was parked outside and I checked my phone as soon as I got into the car. I had a message.

Dylan: Have a good day, babe. I love you xxx

Tears fell silently down my face as I tried to keep my composure while the wheels in my head kept turning and turning and turning, running through every worst case scenario possible. I was immediately brought back to Edward's final days, and I began convincing myself that I was about to go through that same hell with my boyfriend, losing myself in painful memories that felt all too familiar.

I held his hand until the ambulance arrived and I tried to keep him talking, to keep him conscious. I was terrified that if I stopped, he would slip away and I would lose him forever. The paramedics asked me to move out of the way and I did, but it was agonising. I looked on as they manoeuvred my brother, lifting him onto a stretcher and into the ambulance. They let me go with him in the back, and I sat silently crying while they continued to do everything they could to save him.

There was a puddle of blood where he had lain in

the road and as we pulled away, I caught a glimpse of the driver who had hit him, wrapped in a blanket and sobbing into his hands. I wanted to be angry at him, wanted to blame him for what had happened to my brother. But I couldn't because I knew that wasn't true. He'd had no more control over what happened than Edward and all I could feel for the man was sympathy.

At the hospital, Edward was whisked away from me before I could say a word, and a nurse ushered me towards the Intensive Care Unit's waiting room. One of the receptionists asked me if I wanted to call anyone and I just handed her my phone, knowing that there was no way I could get the words out to our parents. They arrived within half an hour, but to me it felt like a full day had passed. I walked up and down the hallway so much that if there had been a carpet I would have worn a line in it.

Mum was beside herself, sobbing and shaking when she arrived. Dad was calmer and pulled me into a hug immediately, but I struggled to return it. I couldn't focus on them. All I could think of was my twin, lying on an operating table suffering God knew what on his own. I couldn't sit still; I was anxious, tetchy and desperate. When Edward finally came out of surgery, I went to see him as soon as I was allowed and planted myself in the chair next to his bed. I stayed in the hospital night and day for the next three days until I had no brother to sit next to.

I was so exhausted I didn't even notice the alarms at first. Doctors rushed in and a nurse ushered me from the room. I realised that something bad was happening and I struggled against her, crying and begging her to let me stay with Edward. I screamed at my twin that I loved him and he wasn't allowed to leave me but it was no use. I was wrangled out of the room and the nurse kept an arm around me as I watched my brother die through the window. I sobbed and snivelled into the stranger's shoulder, and she comforted me, despite my earlier manic behaviour.

I went back into Edward's room, where I stayed until my parents arrived. I didn't want to move but I knew that I should give them some time alone with their son, or what was left of him. I sat in the waiting room, unashamedly still crying. There were others there but we were all in a similar situation, so we minded our own business without judging one another. I was sure that room had seen thousands of outbursts over the years. Mum and Dad came out to meet me and we went home after I'd been back in to say goodbye. I left before they pulled the sheet over him, not wanting to see the white shape covering him. I was silent all the way home, my tears dried out and my throat raw from my continuous sobs. There was only one person I wanted to talk to, to take comfort from, and he was gone.

Chapter Twenty-Four

It didn't take long for Flo to get us to the hospital. I'm pretty sure she didn't stop at a single light and I wasn't sure if that was because we were lucky or because she broke multiple laws to get us there. I really wasn't paying enough attention to notice. I knew she was trying to speak to me in the car but it was like my head was underwater and everything was muffled. I might as well have been blind when we went into the hospital because I couldn't have told you which entrance we used or what turns we took. Hell, I didn't even know what floor we were on. All I knew was that the waiting room was bringing with it familiar feelings of fear, anxiety and hopelessness.

After what felt like hours, a doctor finally found us and explained what had happened.

"My name is Doctor Perry. I'm so sorry to keep you waiting. Dylan was involved in an accident. A gas pipe exploded and he has suffered significant third degree burns to his face and neck. We've checked him over and treated the wounds but there will be scarring."

"Can we see him?" I asked, my mind boggled by all the information that was being hurled at me. I needed to see him, so I knew that he was still here. Flo squeezed my hand and I squeezed back. I knew from experience that she must be desperate for the same thing.

"You can. He's awake. We just wanted to let you know what had happened so that it was less of a shock."

We followed the doctor to Dylan's private room. There were curtains drawn around the bed, and it took all of my willpower not to sprint ahead and pull them back. I hated the idea of walls and curtains and people being between us.

The doctor left us at the door and I was about to

go in when a soft tug on my hand held me back. "I think you should go in without me," Flo whispered behind me.

I turned, confused. "Why?"

"He'll need you more than he'll need me," she told me. "I know I'm his sister, but you're his whole world. He needs to know that you're still here with him."

"Are you sure?"

"Absolutely. I'll be in the waiting room."

I watched Flo turn but I was already through the door before she'd taken her first step. I couldn't wait any longer. I was desperate to see him, to touch him, to put my mind at ease that he was okay. He was turned away from the door but when he heard my heels on the linoleum floor, he looked around and I was relieved to see him awake and alert. I rushed across the room to his bedside and placed my hand in his, using the other to stroke the uncovered side of his face.

"Are you okay?" His eyes were tight with needless worry.

"You're in a hospital bed with half your face covered in bandages and you're asking me if I'm okay?" I laughed, shaking my head and trying to hold back the ridiculous tears that were forming in my eyes. I kissed him, gently, terrified of doing anything that would cause him pain.

"Sit down," he croaked. "We should talk." I stiffened but did as he said, pulling the plastic chair to his bedside. "The doctors have said that I have a long recovery ahead of me and that I'm going to come out the other side with some pretty aggressive scarring." I nodded. "It's going to be a lot, and…" He stopped and swallowed. My heart felt like it was going to burst through my chest waiting for him to finish his thought. "I don't want you to feel like you have to stay with me. You've been through so much already and I don't want to make your life harder."

I couldn't believe what I was hearing. This man was lying in a hospital bed, with horrendous facial burns, and he was worried about me having a hard time.

"Dylan, that is the stupidest thing that has ever come out of your mouth, and that's impressive given some of the shit you've said to me." I shuffled my chair as close to his bed as I could so that we were practically nose to nose. I needed him to hear what I was about to say. "I am not going anywhere. I love you far too much to let you go."

I felt Dylan's hand reach around the back of my head, holding me in place, and his lips hit mine in a rough, possessive kiss that all at once claimed me and showed me how scared he'd been, thinking I might take the way out he had offered me. His lips slowed but I made no effort to move away, feeling a need to stay close.

"I love you too, baby."

Chapter Twenty-Five

I stepped outside to call Angela and update her on what had happened, which gave Flo time to see her brother and have some privacy. I knew how scary it was to go through something like that with your sibling, and I wanted them to have all the time they needed together.

It took a week for Dylan to come out of hospital. A week of monitoring and wound cleaning that eventually began to get on his nerves. The nurse had talked me through how to help him care for the wounds he'd sustained and what to expect over the next few weeks, and he had a follow up appointment in a month to assess whether anything could be done to help the healing process.

While it was good to know that so much medical support was available, Dylan wasn't looking that far ahead yet. We hadn't really talked about how we would deal with the fallout of his injuries. Whenever it came up in conversation, he would find some way to change the subject. I knew it would have to be discussed eventually but the last thing I wanted was to make him uncomfortable or upset, so I decided to let it go for the time being.

One thing that couldn't be let go, though, was his living situation. The doctors had made it very clear that they were concerned about him being on his own and he seemed worried about it, too. While he was desperate to leave the hospital, he also looked conflicted whenever the topic of going home came up.

"You're going to need someone on hand at any time for a while because if you feel ill or in too much pain, someone needs to be able to bring you in," the nurse told him firmly before glancing pointedly at me. "Is that going to be an issue?" Dylan wouldn't look at me, keeping his gaze firmly on the nurse.

"I'm not sure. I can probably work something out," he told her, in a tone that I didn't trust.

"Live with me," I blurted out, without a second thought.

"What?" He turned to me, nearly giving himself whiplash. The nurse must have sensed that this was a private moment as she discreetly excused herself.

"I don't want to be a burden," he said quietly, not looking me in the eye.

"Why would my boyfriend living with me be a burden?"

"Well, it's not going to be easy with me recovering."

"I don't care. I want you to live with me. Do you not want to?" I held my breath, worried that I had read our relationship completely wrong.

"Of course I do! I would love to live with you but I don't want you to do this just because you feel bad."

"I'm not. I promise," I told him, squeezing his hands. "I love having you around. I love you. I would love you to live with me."

I saw him searching my face for any trace of doubt but I knew in my heart that he wouldn't find any. I stroked down the unbandaged side of his face and shuffled closer to him.

"So, do you want to live with me?"

He rubbed his nose against mine and I closed my eyes, savouring the connection. "Yes, I want to live with you."

Angela had already dropped Iggy off by the time we got home and my key was on the doormat after being posted through the letterbox. I could've collected it from the office but I was taking the next week off and then working from home indefinitely after that so I could help Dylan in his recovery. I opened the fridge to make us a brew and found a dish of casserole with a sticky note that said *Love Ange xxx*. She really was an angel. I made a mental note to send her flowers and some other treats to show my appreciation.

When I went back to the living room, Dylan was on the couch with his legs up and Iggy was on his lap, licking the blanket that was over him. I perched myself on the arm of the couch after handing him his mug, and tried to assess him. He looked like he was okay, burn aside, obviously. But he didn't look like he was in pain which was my biggest worry. He caught me watching him and stuck his tongue out, making me smile and relax slightly.

"Come sit with me," he urged, lifting Iggy off his lap so that we could curl up together. I leant against him, luxuriating in the feeling of warmth and safety. I'd been home alone all week and I'd missed him like crazy.

I'd struggled to sleep the whole time he'd been in the hospital and I could feel it catching up with me as I finally slowed down. Dylan took the cup from my hands and began stroking my hair. I tried to keep my eyes open and focus on the television but it was a lost cause and I succumbed to sleep within minutes.

When I woke up, the room had gone dark and I could tell by the gentle movement of his chest that Dylan was asleep, too. I stayed where I was, not ready to move away from him just yet. I was more relaxed than I'd been all week and I had no inclination to bring the moment to an end. Unfortunately, my stomach had other ideas and growled insanely loudly. I let out a little chuckle that woke Dylan up, and he wrapped his arms around my waist, squeezing me gently. I let out a soft hum and placed my hands over his, intertwining our fingers. I knew I should get up and make tea but I was so beyond comfortable in his arms that I didn't want to move ever again.

Our first night back together in bed was lush. We went up early and watched a film in comfort, with the heating on and plenty of blankets. We stayed awake for hours, not saying much but just holding each other. I was still thanking my lucky stars that he was still here with me after I'd been so convinced I would lose him. The thought of him dying never knowing just how much I loved him had terrified me and I was determined to make sure I told him, every day for the rest of our lives.

When I woke up, Dylan was already sitting up against the headboard with dark circles under his bloodshot eyes. I quickly looked him up and down, trying to see if there was any problem that I could immediately fix.

"What's wrong?"

"Nothing, I just didn't sleep much. I can't lie on my side right now," he explained, rubbing his eyes and flinching as he hit the bandages on the left of his face. They were definitely in need of changing and I decided to make that priority number one of the day.

"Let me sort out your dressings, then we'll get breakfast and see about finding you something that'll help you sleep," I suggested, punctuating my words with a kiss. Iggy was still snoozing on the bed so we moved around him and wandered off to the bathroom.

Dylan sat on the edge of the bath, bracing himself while I peeled the gauze from his face. I was glad I was wearing gloves because it wasn't the neatest process in the world. I knew what to expect. I'd done plenty of research and the nurse had told me what to look out for to avoid infection. I put the used bandages in the bin and grabbed the antiseptic wipes. Dylan flinched as I cleaned his face and I hated that I was hurting him. I managed to get rid of the gunk that was covering the burn and let it dry out before I put on any ointment and further bandages. It didn't look great but not in an *oh my God that's ugly* way—more in an *oh my God that looks insanely painful and I have no idea how you aren't absolutely screaming at me for touching it* kind of way. But in terms of how he looked himself, it was nothing. He was still the most handsome thing I'd ever laid eyes on and I still wanted to kiss him all over but when he asked for a mirror, I was reluctant to hand it over. I knew that it didn't bother me yet I was worried that it would be an issue for him. I didn't want him to feel self conscious.

"Are you sure you want to see?"

"Not really, but I should probably know what's going on under there," he told me with a grimace. I grabbed a mirror and sat on the edge of the bath with him before I handed it over. I placed my hand on his thigh, ready to deal with any reaction that came, but for a long moment he didn't say anything. I was just starting to relax when he turned to me. "How can you look at me?" I looked deep into his eyes and saw agony, insecurity and doubt as well as something else I didn't have a name for that hurt my soul.

"What do you mean?"

"How can you stand to look at this? I'm horrific," he huffed, and turned away from me but not fast enough for me to miss the glisten of unshed tears in his eyes. I took the mirror from his hands and moved around to stand between his legs, holding his chin in my hand so he had no choice but to look at me.

"This is not forever," I reminded him. "You will heal, but even if you didn't, it wouldn't make a shred of difference. You'll always be gorgeous to me." He sniffed and didn't say anything but I felt doubt in his silence. "Stop over thinking. You're upsetting yourself over something that isn't a problem." I traced my finger tips down the untouched side of his face and kissed his lips, softly to avoid hurting him but, I hoped, with enough pressure to show him that I still adored every inch of him.

I dabbed ointment onto his skin and redressed it as delicately as I could, not wanting him to be in any more pain than he must already have been in. He didn't say anything as I finished up but after I'd put everything away, he pulled me back between his thighs and crushed me to him, resting the undamaged part of his face on my stomach. I wove my fingers into his hair, my nails dragging across his scalp, and I saw goosebumps erupt over his bare shoulders. I loved that even at a time like this, I could still have that effect on him and I smiled to myself as a guttural moan came from the back of his throat.

"I don't know what I ever did to deserve you," he mumbled.

"Clearly, you misbehaved in a previous life and I am your punishment," I teased with a giggle, but when he looked up at me his eyes were full of sincerity.

"Seriously, you're amazing, you know that?"

"Nope, but please feel free to continue telling me." I winked at him before pulling him to his feet so we could go and have breakfast. He smiled but it didn't reach his eyes, and I hoped that his mood would pick up as the day went on.

While I was making breakfast, I could hear Dylan on the phone to Flo in the living room, reassuring her that he was fine. I knew that she would text me later on to check in again for an honest answer. I knew Dylan wasn't lying to be an arsehole or anything; he just didn't want to worry her and that was nice, but he needed to be honest so that he didn't implode and self-destruct. I hoped that if the morning was anything to go by, he would at least keep being honest with me.

When he came through to the kitchen, he seemed

somewhat happier after speaking to his sister. We sat and ate while Iggy did laps around and under the kitchen table, whining and yapping to go out for his walk. We'd woken up late and he wasn't used to having to wait this long so he was getting a little impatient. We wrapped up warm, even Iggy put on his little jumper, and we set out to brave the cold so that the little monster would behave for the day. We stopped at our usual park bench so that he could run around like an idiot for twenty or so minutes while we huddled like penguins for warmth.

There weren't many people out as it was eleven in the morning on a weekday, but I could feel Dylan becoming more and more tense with every person we saw and it didn't help that people kept staring. I get it, it's hard not to look when someone has a massive bandage covering nearly half their face but for the love of God at least make some attempt to be subtle. By the time about seven people had passed, Dylan had all but shrunk into himself and I was ready to jump off the bench and fight someone, so we decided to leave and get back to our cosy, safe place.

Feeling that Dylan might need some comfort, I brought the duvet downstairs and arranged us on the couch so that he was between my legs and could rest his head on me without worrying about hurting his face. We flicked on the television and watched some cheesy horror movie from way back when. We were about halfway through when I realised Dylan had fallen asleep on me. One of my legs had also fallen asleep with him lying on it but there was no way I was waking him up so I could move. He was so tired and I wanted him to have as much rest as possible to help him feel better. I looked down at him and thought back to all the support he had given me when I was struggling with my feelings. How good he had been with me when I really didn't deserve him and how much care and attention he'd given me when I needed it the most. I vowed to myself, and to him, that I would be everything he could possibly need to get him through this.

Chapter Twenty-Six

I wasn't surprised when Dylan didn't want to walk Iggy with me after that first time. He also hadn't seen Flo since his bandages had come off, not wanting her to know the extent of the damage. He'd even tried to hide it from me but there was no way in hell I was having that.

It was subtle at first. He would conveniently place himself on my right so that I could only see the left side of his face, or he would turn me around so that I wasn't looking at him when he hugged me. I finally snapped and confronted him when he woke up a few weeks after he'd come home and saw me, already awake and facing him. He flinched away immediately, trying to hide the blistered skin from my sight. I was quicker than him, though, and I straddled him, forcing him to look at me.

"What was that?" I demanded.

"What? Nothing," he mumbled, still trying to turn his face away from me.

Taking care not to hurt him, I slid my hands under his head and knotted my fingers into his hair, holding his head in place. When he finally met my gaze, I saw tears in his eyes and he only looked at me for two seconds before closing his eyes and letting the moisture seep from under his lids.

"Babe, don't..." I could hear the lump in his throat and my heart cracked for him.

"Don't what?"

"I don't want you to have to see it," he whispered, sorrow seeping through every syllable. His hands were quaking on my thighs and his chest was heaving as he tried to hold back the agony he felt inside.

"Dylan, please look at me," I begged, my own tears at risk of breaking through. I waited until he opened his eyes before I spoke to him. I needed to know that he was taking in every word. "No amount of blisters, or scarring, or injury will ever stop me wanting to look at you," I whispered, my voice cracking on the final word. "You will always be the most perfect thing in my world."

He shook his head, not accepting what I was trying to say, and I tried not to get frustrated with him. It wasn't his fault—not at all—but it was hard knowing I was speaking from the deepest part of me and that he couldn't hear it through the walls he'd built up around himself. I wiped the tears from the parts of his face I could touch without hurting him, and leant down so that my chest was pressed against him. I moved myself so that I had his head cocooned in my arms and felt him bury his face in my neck. The sobs that came from him were from weeks of pent up anger, frustration, anxiety and insecurity. He clung to me like his life depended on it, as if I was about to vanish into thin air.

When his tears subsided they were replaced with words that made me clutch him even tighter: "I'm sorry. I love you. Stay with me. I need you."

I felt tortured by his insecurities so I could only imagine how he was feeling. I touched him, kissed him, whispered reassurances and words of love to him. Time stopped existing and the only thing present, aside from the two of us, was the intense need to put his fears to rest and let him know that I was completely and unquestionably his.

His whispers turned to worshipping kisses, nips and licks that hit my neck in just the right places. I ground my hips against his erection, needing friction to ease the ache between my legs that he had brought on. I felt him buck against me and a wicked grin twitched at my lips, loving that he was just as pent up as I was.

It had been almost a month since we'd touched each other this way. I hadn't instigated anything because I was terrified to do anything that might cause him pain, but feeling that he was here with me spurred me on. His hand flared at the base of my spine, crushing us together. He sunk his teeth into my shoulder and I moaned into his ear, telling him I needed more. I'd fallen asleep in flimsy underwear and he tore them away in seconds. With no fabric between us, I was desperate for him. I raised myself up enough to be able to position him at my entrance and sat so that I could fully sink down onto him. Once I was upright, I saw and felt him freeze. I paused, giving him time to decide whether he wanted to stop what was about to happen. Instead, he turned his head and tried to thrust into me. I moved, lifting my hips to stop him doing what he wanted. His brow furrowed with confusion until I used my fingers to turn his face back to me. He shook his head, trying to evade me.

"Dylan, let me see you."

"You don't want that." He shook his head.

"I promise you, I do, okay?"

He pulled my hand from his face and brought it to his lips. "Okay."

I wasn't usually one to use the term, but I couldn't describe what happened between us as *fucking;* we made love. We bared our souls to each other and I gave him everything I had. I worshipped him, held him close, showered him in affection with my words and my actions. We were in sync together, giving and taking. Every movement was special because it held something real, something important, something *more*.

For the rest of the day we basked in the overwhelming feelings of love, warmth and satisfaction. Everything seemed as well as I could have hoped.

The following day, I finally opened my eyes and looked at the man beside me. He hadn't been able to shave for a while so he was showing the beginnings of a beard. Remembering the way it had felt, rubbing up my chest made me shiver. I must have disturbed him because he stretched out languidly and instinctively turned away when he caught me looking at him.

"Dylan, don't," I begged, my heart sinking. I really thought that our morning before had shown him that I wanted him no matter what, but clearly I hadn't done a good enough job.

"I'm sorry," he whispered as he dragged his fingers down my cheek. "I'm sorry, I don't want to upset you."

I covered his hand with my own and choked back the tears that were threatening to fall. The rational part of my brain knew that this wasn't about me, that this wasn't even really anything to do with me. But the irrational, emotional part of me took his actions to heart and I felt like I'd failed him. I wanted to make all of the insecurities go away—his and mine—but I didn't know how. A drop of moisture fell from my lashes and I took myself off to the bathroom before I lost it completely.

I heard Dylan's footsteps down the hall and tried to gather myself before he reached me. I dabbed the moisture on my face with a tissue and looked in the mirror. Seeing the blotchy mess of my face made me feel even worse. He knocked on the door, gently.

"Babe, can you let me in?"

I took a shaky breath and slid the latch back, granting him access. He was a striking figure, taking up the space in the doorway. His low slung lounge pants gave me a front row view to his muscular chest and the delicious v leading down to his crotch. In a normal situation I would have been jumping his bones right about now but I was far too lost in the turmoil surrounding us. He stepped into the little room and rested his hands on the basin, caging me in between it and him.

"Don't cry. It's not worth crying over."

So, of course, I cried harder. "How could you say that? Of course it's worth crying over. You won't even let me look at you," I wailed and tried to turn in his arms but he held onto the tops of my arms, holding me in place.

"Please, just let me explain," he whispered, his eyes boring into me. "Come on, come back to bed."

He ran downstairs to make us a brew and when he came back up, I was sitting in bed, with tears still wet on my cheeks. I took the mug off him gratefully, letting the warmth seep into my bones. I hadn't bothered to put on a dressing gown when I ran from the bedroom so I was shivering my life away. He put his mug on the bedside table and scooped me up, lifting me onto his lap and wrapping the duvet around us. In spite of my sad mood, I couldn't help but smile a little. It felt like I was stuck in a big marshmallow with my favourite human pressed up against me. Toasty and sweet. He smoothed out my hair and cleared his throat before he began.

"I know I keep trying to stop you looking at me and I know it's upsetting you," he started. "And I really don't want you to think that it's something about you because it absolutely isn't. I get that's how it's coming across from your point of view but I want to try to explain from mine because I didn't do a very good job last time."

"You don't need to explain anything to me. I just need to get my feelings in check and-"

"No. I want to explain, because I can see you taking it personally and that's the exact opposite of how it should be because you are the only thing keeping me going right now. You deserve an explanation."

I nodded and passed him my mug to put on the side with his, so I could wrap my arms around his middle.

"I'm not trying to hide my face from you because I think you'll laugh, or that you'll say something, or that you'll run screaming or anything like that. When I look at you, I see the most perfect person in the world, and then when I look in the mirror, I see someone who doesn't deserve to be with you. In my eyes, someone like you doesn't fit with someone like me. I've always felt it on some level but this has just amplified it and it scares me." I wanted to interrupt him and tell him that he had nothing to worry about but I bit my tongue, hoping that getting this off his chest would do him some good. "I feel so insecure now. You know I haven't left the house in forever. I haven't seen my sister, and it's because I'm terrified of how people are going to react to me."

"How can I help?" I whispered. "How do I make it go away?"

"You can't." He smiled down at me sadly. "You can't work through this for me. It's my own mind doing this. I'm just hoping that you'll still be here when I've figured it out."

I rearranged myself so that I was still on his lap but we were face to face. I nudged his chin up with my nose and kissed up his neck and jawline until I reached his ear.

"I'll always be here Dylan, and I can see your point of view. I don't mean to get upset. I just hate that you feel like you need to hide from me."

"It's not you, I swear. I feel like I should hide from

everyone right now," he mumbled, the words muffled as he pressed his face into my hair.

"That's so ridiculous." I felt him stiffen, and when I looked up, his expression was incredulous.

"Eren, look at me. Half of my face is messed up. I'm... repulsive. You shouldn't have to see that."

"I wish you could see yourself the way I see you." I sniffled. "You're the brightest thing in my life. Every time I look at you I get all warm and fuzzy inside. You could come home one day with no face whatsoever and I would still think you were insanely hot. I thought, maybe, yesterday had shown you that..." I trailed off, embarrassed at how ridiculous I sounded.

He cupped my face with both of his hands and I leant into him involuntarily. "Yesterday was incredible. I'm still blown away by it and I'll never, ever forget the way you looked at me. It was like I was your whole world."

"Because you are!"

"But that doesn't stop my brain working overtime and ruining things for me."

I understood. I knew myself what it was like when you shut out the intrusive thoughts and I had an idea.

"If this was the other way around and I was feeling this way, what would you say to me?"

"I would tell you that I love you and that I'm not

going anywhere... and I would probably suggest that you restart your counselling."

I caressed his lips with mine and looked him dead in his periwinkle eyes. "Dylan..." He shook his head and smiled wryly, knowing exactly what I was going to say before I said it. "I love you and I'm not going anywhere, and I think you should consider counselling."

"Will you come with me?"

"Of course I will, babe. I'll be right by your side the whole time," I promised.

"Okay, then I'll do it."

Chapter Twenty-Seven

We made it to see Dylan's counsellor. I had arranged the appointment over the phone but when it came to getting him out of the house, things got difficult. Excuse after excuse was made to prevent walking through that front door. Would Iggy be okay on his own for a couple of hours? Was I sure I was okay driving in the rain? Did we have enough petrol to get us there? It was like pulling teeth, but I eventually got him into the waiting room. With his hood up, he clung to my hand as soon as we were out of the car and I was sure by the time we left again I would need the bones in it resetting.

At the front desk, he froze up and I had to get him signed in for his appointment. I could feel his hand getting clammier by the second and his breathing was becoming more and more laboured. When the counsellor called his name, he jumped out of his skin and looked at me, his eyes bulging in panic. I pulled him off the chair and flashed the counsellor a look that I hope explained the situation.

"Babe, it's time to go in," I told him, my voice soft and calming.

"You're coming with me, right?"

"Of course, I'll be with you as long as you need." I smiled encouragingly.

"The whole time—you have to stay the whole time." He squeezed my hand again, even harder than before.

"Okay, I'll be there the whole time, I promise."

The doctor's office was a very light room with white furniture and lots of knick knacks that gave every surface a pop of colour. I found the decor to have a very calm vibe but Dylan was still rigid beside me.

"My name is Dianne," the doctor told us as she closed the door. She kept her distance as we made our introductions, and I was grateful that she allowed

Dylan to have his space while he was in such a temperamental state.

"Why don't you both take a seat?"

The layout of the room meant that Dylan couldn't hide his left side from her and I could tell that it was stressing him out. We sat on the couch and Dylan pulled me into him so that we were touching. I rested my hand on his thigh in an effort to reassure him and keep him grounded. He still hadn't introduced himself so I did it for him.

"This is Dylan and I'm Eren. Thank you for seeing us today."

"My pleasure." She smiled before deliberately making direct eye contact with Dylan. "I know that I briefly discussed your situation with Eren over the phone but would you be able to explain in your own words why you're here?"

I heard Dylan swallow next to me and I leant my weight onto him ever so slightly, giving him an encouraging smile.

"I was recently injured in a minor gas explosion," he mumbled. "Now I can't go out of the house or see anyone because of my face. Just getting here was hell."

"Because of your face?" Dianne probed.

"Because I don't want anyone to see it."

"That's why you still have your hood up?"

Dylan nodded. "No one needs to see that mess,"

I sniffled beside him, trying to keep my emotions in check. He needed me to be strong but it never got any easier to hear him speak so lowly of himself.

"What about Eren?"

"What about her?"

"Do you feel the same way about her seeing you as you do everyone else?"

"Yes," he told her, looking at me with doleful eyes. "I hate that she has to wake up to *this* every day."

"Has she ever given you a reason to think she feels that way?"

The idea gave me pause and I wondered whether Dylan had ever seen anything in me that made him feel insecure.

"No, never. She's so loving and patient, much more so than I deserve."

It was strange hearing them talk about me as if I wasn't there, but I had expected this to be the case so I was surprised when Dianne looked to me for an opinion.

"Eren, do you have any negative feelings about waking up with him everyday?"

"No," I told her instantly, before turning to meet his eyes. "Not a single one. I want to wake up to him every single day for the rest of my life." I could hear

Dianne's pen scratching on her notepad but I didn't take my eyes off my man. I was desperate for him to see how much I meant every word I said.

We were in the office for an hour but Dianne didn't ask any more deep questions. It was more of a getting to know you session than anything else. She asked about his family, his work, his hobbies and our life at home. Although still uncomfortable, Dylan relaxed ever so slightly by the time his appointment was up and he booked another session for the following week, with Dianne's blessing to bring me along again.

"I'm sorry. I know it's pathetic," he stammered once we were in the car.

"No, it's not," I contested, my hand reaching out for him while I kept my eyes on the road ahead of me. "It's perfectly fine to want support when you're doing something that's emotionally exhausting. I'll come with you for as many sessions as you want."

Dylan was wrung out that afternoon; being honest and emotionally vulnerable was an exhausting task and he was definitely feeling it. He fell asleep on me again so that he wouldn't hurt his face, and I scratched my nails gently on his scalp until I heard him start to snore.

I was mindlessly scrolling on my phone when a message popped up from Flo.

Flo: How was it? Is he okay?

Eren: It was good. He's fine but exhausted so he's fallen asleep on me. He's going again next week.

Flo: On his own?

Eren: He wants me to go with him but he might change his mind once the day comes. We'll just have to wait and see.

Flo: Do you think he'll let me see him soon?

I let out a huff and looked down at Dylan's sleeping form. I wished at that moment that I could read his mind and then maybe I would stand a chance of giving Flo a half decent answer.

Eren: I don't know. I hope so.

I didn't press him about Flo when he woke up, anticipating that he would still be feeling tender from his session today. He woke up when I had to hold his arm to stop him scratching at his face, and he looked at me with a guilty expression.

"Sorry, I didn't realise I was doing that."

"Of course you didn't. You were asleep," I

reminded him. "I just wanted to make sure you didn't hurt yourself. That's all."

"It's so itchy. It's like a million mites are trying to burrow into my skin." I leant forward to press a kiss onto the top of his head, inhaling his woodsy scent as I did.

"I'm sorry, baby. I wish I could do something to help."

He weaved his fingers between mine and rubbed his thumb in circles on the top of my hand. "Don't be sorry. It's not your fault. I just feel disgusting." The self loathing had returned to his usually gentle tone and it made me sad as it did every time.

"Well, I still think you're fit as fuck." I grinned at him. My comment earned me a chuckle before he lifted himself onto his knees and kissed me.

"You're adorable, but I still feel gross."

I let out a puff of breath and pushed him off me. I saw a flicker of rejection and hurt in his eyes but it was quickly replaced by confusion when I stood up and held my hand out to him. "Come on, we're going for a bath."

The bath was exactly what we needed. The water was that perfect temperature that makes you feel like you're floating in heaven. The bath salts had evaporated, leaving behind a scent of bergamot and lemongrass, and I played some classical music on my phone to help us unwind. Iggy had come in to inspect the room but left very quickly to go somewhere cooler, leaving us to have a completely private moment.

I sat between Dylan's legs and rested my head against his chest. We sat in silence for a long time, me with my hands resting on his athletic legs and him stroking my hair with one hand and keeping the other firmly around my waist. I'd noticed that since his accident, Dylan felt the need to make physical contact with me as much as possible despite also trying to hide his face. His two compulsions were at odds with one another and I wondered about the constant battle that must be raging in his head. I wanted to ask and I toyed around with the question in my mind before I let it spill out.

"Why do you touch me so much?" *Smooth, nice one, Eren*.

"What?"

"I've noticed that since you got hurt, you've

become more touchy feely with me. I was wondering why." I felt him tense behind me and mentally berated myself for letting my curiosity get the better of me.

"Is it a problem for you?" His voice wavered and I felt my heart ache.

"Not at all, I love it," I reassured him swiftly. "I was just interested to know where it came from." I shrugged. "Forget I said anything."

"No, it's okay. I'll tell you." He rested his chin on my shoulder. "I guess, part of it is that if anything I've fallen even more in love with you since everything happened, which I didn't even think was possible."

"And the other part?"

"The other part is that I think I'm still waiting for you to leave, and having physical contact with you reminds me that you're still here and helps push down some of the crazy I've got going on in my head." His words came out in a hap hazard, jagged way and I could feel the tension in the air as he waited for my response.

"I can see how that makes sense," I told him, and I felt him unclench. "But I'm not going anywhere, whether we're touching each other or not." I don't know if it was the atmosphere of honesty, whether he was too tired to edit himself or whether the stress of the whole day brought it out of him, but he gave me a further insight into his thoughts.

"I hope you stay around. I *need* you to stay around. You're my lifeline. If you had left me, I wouldn't have blamed you, but it would have destroyed me. I know that it's unfair for me to put that kind of pressure on you and I'd still understand now if you left me. But I don't know how or if I would ever recover from that..." He trailed off and I was terrified of the dark turn his thoughts were taking.

"You'll never have to worry about that, ever," I told him firmly, turning myself over as much as I could so that we were face to face. In my haste to make eye contact with him, I splashed water all over the bathroom floor but I really didn't give a shit. "There's no reason for you to even consider that as a possibility." His hand came up to move a stray hair that had drifted onto my face and I leant my face into his palm.

"I hate that I think like that but I can't help it. It just sneaks up on me."

"I can understand that. Intrusive thoughts are a bitch. Maybe your counselling will help with that."

"I hope so. I don't want my bullshit fucking up what we have."

"We're a team, babe. Your bullshit is my bullshit. We'll deal with it together, and when we're sat together on our front porch all old and wrinkly, you'll wonder why you were ever worried."

"I love that you plan on us growing old together," he whispered, kissing the hollow under my ear.

"Of course I do. I'm keeping you, forever."

Chapter Twenty-Eight

"Babe?"

"Yeah, hon?" I asked without opening my eyes, knowing that as soon as the light hit them I wouldn't be able to go back to sleep.

"Are you awake?"

"No. Do you need me to be?"

"Maybe," he mumbled. "I don't know."

I wrenched back my lids and looked at the alarm clock—five o'clock in the morning. This was unholy. I rolled over so my head was resting on his chest and I entwined my legs with his. "What's up?"

"Flo messaged me and I don't know what to do." He handed me his phone and I squinted against the blaring light to read the message.

Flo: I know this is hard for you but it's hard for me, too, and you're really hurting my feelings by not letting me see you. Why is it that you can see Eren but not me? What's wrong with me? She said it was because you felt insecure about your face and I accepted that, but now it's getting ridiculous. You're my brother. I want to see you. Please let me.

I groaned and passed the phone back to him. "It's too early for this bullshit."

"Sorry." I felt his lips moving my hair.

"No, it's not your fault." I moved so I was sitting up next to him against the headboard. "Are you wanting to reply or not?"

"I don't know. I feel like I should because she's my sister and I love her, but also it's like, I'm working hard to get myself into a better place where I can see her without all these negative feelings about myself cropping up and she needs to respect that it's a process. But I don't want her to be upset so maybe I should just do it and suck it up when I feel like shit."

I was shaking my head before he'd even finished the thought. "No! I'm sorry but no," I told him firmly. "Your recovery process is about you. She needs to work to your timeline, not the other way around. Remember what Dianne said."

"No one is entitled to your time, space or energy," he recited, and I nodded along with him, glad he had been taking it in.

"You go at your own pace, no one else's. You will see her when you're ready."

"So what do I say?" he asked, chewing on his lip.

"You say, *Flo, I love you but I'm not ready yet. I'm in counselling and I need to focus on* my *feelings right now, not anybody else's. I don't want to upset you but I need to do what's best for me.*"

I rested my head on his shoulder as he typed out the message to his sister, and I tried not to sit and stew in my own feelings. It was tough not to message Flo myself and ask her what the hell she thought she was doing. How dare she try to emotionally manipulate him into seeing her when he wasn't ready? She knew how hard he was trying to get his head sorted and then decided she was going to try to force him to rush it because *she* was upset? Unacceptable. It was hard to see it play out, and part of it was because I could imagine how Edward and I would have reacted in this situation.

I would have thought that if Edward were in Dylan's shoes, he would still want to see me, but then again, we were living together and we had always been close. I bit my tongue, not wanting to say anything to Dylan that would stress him out more than he already was. I didn't want to be a source of anxiety in his life.

He sent his message and put his phone back on the bedside table. He pulled me back down the mattress and shifted me into a spooning position. He ran his fingers up and down my arms, trying to pull me back into sleep.

"I'm sorry I woke you up," he whispered.

"Mmmhmm, you're lucky it's Saturday and I don't have to get up and work," I teased him, scooching myself closer into his body.

"I'll make it up to you with breakfast later," he promised, before sleep took me.

Breakfast was worth the early wake up call. It seemed Dylan had been hiding some skills from me because those pancakes were so good it had me drooling before I'd even started eating them.

"Oh my God, you need to make these every day for

me forever!"

Dylan eventually agreed to come with me to walk Iggy, for the first time in forever. We didn't go far and he kept his hood up the entire time, shielding most of his face from view. It should have upset me that he felt the need to do that but I was just so thrilled that he had finally agreed to go for a walk with me that I couldn't bring myself to be bothered by it.

After walking a couple of blocks, I could tell Dylan was starting to get twitchy so we walked back home to do some afternoon yoga before being lazy for the evening. I was very conscious of falling out of practice while I was staying at home, and Dylan was more than happy to help me continue it at home, using 'correcting my posture' as an excuse to put his hands all over me. I was *very* receptive and made deliberate mistakes, playing right into his hands in the hopes that it would give him a confidence boost. And also, just because I liked his attention. We were happily doing our cool down, sitting on the floor in silence, clearing our minds and centering ourselves when there was an aggressive knock on the door. Dylan's panicked eyes met my confused ones and I jumped up to answer it. When I opened the door, Flo's face was directly in front of mine and I saw red.

"Please don't be mad," she implored me, reading

my facial expression immediately. "I'm desperate to see him." She tried to step into the hallway and I blocked her way.

"What the hell do you think you're doing?"

"Eren, please, he's my brother. I miss him. You know what that's like," she whined, hoping to garner my sympathy. It was the wrong thing to say.

"That is not the same thing. My brother is dead. I will never, ever see him again." My voice shook with fury. "You will see your brother again when he's ready. You're being completely unfair."

"But if it was you and Edward-"

"Don't you dare. Don't you dare try to use that as an excuse to disrespect Dylan's boundaries." My voice was getting louder and louder, and I heard Dylan shout to me from the front room.

"Eren, what's going on?" I tried to let out a calming exhale so my stress wouldn't carry over to him.

"Your sister is here."

There was silence. I waited for his response, tense and stiff. Flo was no better. I looked at her and her face was apologetic, as if she had suddenly realised this was a bad idea. I pinched the bridge of my nose and sighed.

"Wait there," I instructed her, closing the front door on her. I went back to the front room and Dylan was standing in the middle of the room, stock still, a horrified look on his face. I rushed to him and put my hands on his shoulders. "Take a breath. It's okay," I told him, meeting his stare. "You don't have to see her. It was unfair for her to come here in the first place and spring this on you."

"I'll come to the door," he whispered. "But she can't come in and it won't be for long. Just, don't leave me alone there, okay?"

"Of course."

We walked to the front door and I opened it again. Dylan's arm tightened around me as the door moved, and as soon as Flo saw him she let out a dramatic gasp. Her hand flew to her mouth and I could have smacked her for it. I felt Dylan crumple beside me; any shred of confidence he'd had died within him and he sagged into me once he had slammed the door shut in his sister's horrified face.

I could hear Flo weeping through the door and I didn't want Dylan to be affected by it, so I flicked the locks back on and pulled him away, sweeping through the living room and going upstairs to the bedroom. He let me drag him along, putting up no resistance and clinging to me the whole way as if I were the only thing keeping him upright.

I sat on the bed and pulled him with me. His head had sunk to his chest as soon as the door had closed and still hadn't moved. I got up onto my knees and wrapped my arms around his broad shoulders. He was clearly upset but he didn't cry, he didn't shout, he didn't do anything. In a way, that was worse. He was just blank, lifeless. Empty. It worried me and I tried to get something out of him by asking if he was okay.

"She looked at me like I was a monster," he mumbled into my shoulder, the heat of his breath warming me. "She'll never look at me normally again."

"She will. She was just surprised, that's all." I tried to defend her. I was still angry but I didn't want him to lose his relationship with his sister completely.

"That right there," he said, lifting his head to look at me. "That face she made is the exact reason why I shouldn't see anyone. I've been right the whole time."

"No, that's not true. Please don't let this set you back."

"How can anything set me back when I haven't actually got anywhere? I'm still a complete and utter mess. You should be running for the hills because all I'm going to do is drag you down with me."

It killed me that he spoke of himself that way and I really did blame Flo for his negative turn. I was livid that she'd ruined everything he'd worked so hard for.

"I'm not going anywhere, you know that," I told him, pressing my forehead to his. He tried to respond but I pressed my lips to his, not giving him a chance to say anything further. I didn't want him to say anything that would bring him further down. He responded to me instantly, his lips moving with mine. His strong arms snaked around my waist and I felt a neediness in his kiss that I'd never felt before. His hands were balled into fists, pulling the fabric of my t-shirt as if he was trying to keep me in place, not that I had any intention of going anywhere.

Flo messaged again that night with an apology.

Flo: I'm so sorry for today. I never wanted to upset you or push you and I know that's exactly what I did. I don't expect you to be ready to speak to me again yet but I needed to say I love you and again, I'm sorry.

It took a long time for Dylan to calm down after Flo's unexpected arrival. We still had our film night but there was a dark cloud hanging over him. He didn't say much for the rest of the evening and I could see that he was withdrawing back into his shell. It hurt to see him that way after he'd made such progress but I was confident that he would come out of it stronger than before.

Chapter Twenty-Nine

Dylan didn't message Flo back for a good few days. I couldn't say I blamed him to be honest. The way she'd acted was selfish and when I told him how she'd tried to use Edward to soften me up, he flipped from upset to angry. He brought it up with Dianne and I was glad when she validated his feelings and reminded him that it was okay to set boundaries, even with people he loved and who loved him.

I was still in on his sessions and he still spent the

whole time with at least one hand on me, but I didn't speak. He needed the space to say whatever he wanted to without me influencing him. Dianne suggested during their fifth session that perhaps I should wait outside for him, but Dylan shut down the idea immediately. It was very bittersweet. While I was happy that I helped him, he needed to learn how to handle his issues independently. I was due to go back to the office soon and I was concerned that he wasn't going to cope. That thought had me debating whether I should work from home permanently, but I missed my office. I missed my colleagues, and my clients missed being able to come for face-to-face meetings with me. I knew I needed to broach the topic with Dylan and I decided to do so over dinner that night.

I sat, picking at the garlic bread on my plate as I tried to think of a sensitive way to bring up the issue of my going back to work. I worked hard trying to keep my face a blank mask so that Dylan wouldn't pick up on my worry. I had underestimated how well he could read me, though, because within five minutes he was asking me what was wrong.

"Don't freak out," I told him, tapping his foot

with mine under the table. "But I need to talk to you about work."

"What about work? You work from home." His brow furrowed and I worried that this conversation would end in tears although I couldn't predict whose.

"I do at the moment, but I would like to go back into the office at some point."

His face dropped and he tensed as if expecting a physical blow. "You're getting fed up with me," he muttered, nodding his head. "I expected this to happen eventually. I hoped I'd have a little more time."

I got up and walked around the table to stand behind him, my plate of pasta forgotten. I put my arms over his shoulders and he instinctively lifted his hands to meet mine.

"It's not that. I love being here with you, but I miss my colleagues. Angela's having to do extra to cover me not being there and my clients are starting to get antsy because I haven't been seeing them."

No response.

"I wouldn't have to go back full time. I could just do two days a week at first and do the rest at home, and we can reassess in a couple of months. You might find you like having some space from me." I chuckled, trying to lighten the tense mood.

"No, I won't." I felt him straighten beneath me

and he twisted his head to face me. "But I don't want to stop you doing a job that you love, and it isn't fair for you to be trapped in the house just because I am."

"I'm not *trapped* here. I just need to make sure that I'm keeping somewhat of a physical presence with my clients, otherwise I'll lose them and then I'll be buggered."

"I get that, really." He squeezed my hands and I squeezed back.

"Thank you for understanding. I was thinking I'd do Tuesday and Thursday in the office and the rest from home. Is that okay with you?"

He pulled me around and onto his lap. "You don't need to ask for my permission to work, Eren."

"I know, but I need to know that you'll be okay."

"I'll be fine. I can text you while you're gone anyway, right?" he asked, sheepishly.

"Of course you can. I'll still want to be talking to you anyway," I assured him.

I was glad he had taken it well but part of me was still worried about what I would come home to on my first Tuesday back in the office. I had asked Angela not to schedule any meetings for the first two weeks so that I was available if Dylan needed me, and I had left Iggy at home with him so that he wasn't completely alone. I missed them both something chronic but I was so excited to see Angela. In all honesty, ninety nine percent of Tuesday was taken up by Angela filling me in on all the gossip I had missed. There had been nights out, birthdays, dramatic exits, new starters, it was crazy. It was like high school again, when you'd be off sick one day and that day suddenly became the highlight of everyone else's year.

"So, anyway, we were at the bar and we heard this scuffle behind us. We turned around and there was Gary, having his absolute arse handed to him because it turned out the girl had a boyfriend and he wouldn't take the hint."

"Was he hurt?" I was concerned. Gary was the last person you'd expect to see in a fight.

"Oh no, he was fine. There were no actual punches thrown," she told me, filing her acrylic nails. "The boyfriend just roughed him up a bit and put him on the floor. I'm sure he's telling it differently, though." She laughed and I made a mental note to ask Gary about it at some point and see what he had to say.

Dylan had messaged me a few times—not excessively but enough for me to know that he was anxious for me to come home. I was anxious to go, too, but I forced myself to stay until five o'clock. If I caved and left early I would be setting myself a bad precedent and I didn't want to do that.

At finishing time, I flew out of the door and into my car. It was a miracle I didn't get a ticket with the speed I drove home at. I knew it was reckless but worry was gnawing at my insides and I needed to know that Dylan was okay.

I could hear music blasting as soon as I stepped through the front door and Iggy slid across the laminate flooring to meet me. Scooping him up into my arms, I walked into the living room and found Dylan lying on the couch, eyes closed but obviously awake as he drummed his fingers on his torso. I bent down to kiss him and his eyes flew open as our lips touched. Wrapping his arms around my middle, he pulled me to lie on top of him and exhaled with enough force to ruffle my hair. I could feel his heartbeat through his shirt and it felt faster than I would have expected for someone resting. I was about to ask if he was okay when he spoke.

"I've missed you today."

"I missed you, too. How was it being here without me?" I kept my tone light and airy so he wouldn't feel like I was checking up on him.

"It was fine, mostly. I was going to walk Iggy but I couldn't make it out of the front door without you. That pissed me off," he reflected, and I made a noise of acknowledgement. "I took him to play in the garden instead. He ran around like a lunatic so he should be fine for the rest of the night."

I kicked off my shoes and re-arranged myself around him on the couch so that I was more comfortable. I flung one leg around his waist and rested my head under his collar bone. Listening to his deep breaths pushed away my worries and I could feel myself drifting to sleep. I was out of practice at socialising so it had taken its toll on me. I must have fallen asleep because the next thing I knew, the house was filled with the smell of roast chicken and gravy.

Chapter Thirty

Dianne was pleased to hear that I was back at the office part time and said that it was a good start to work towards Dylan getting back to his old self again. Again, she brought up the possibility of me no longer attending the appointments with him and he promised he would think about it. I saw him tense when it was brought up and I was pretty sure I knew what his thought process would be but I didn't say a word about it, there or at home. I wanted to do everything I could to help him recover, but I wasn't about to start forcing him into things he wasn't comfortable with, so the good doctor would have to grin and bear my presence for a little while longer.

After some more appointments, Dianne raised a persistent concern of hers: Dylan's self esteem issues.

"It's been nearly five months since the accident, and you still haven't spent any time with anyone other than Eren and I. I'd like to talk about why that is."

"You know why. I don't want anyone seeing me," Dylan reminded her, his features hardening.

"I understand that. Let me phrase this differently." She leant forward in her seat and put down her pad and pen. "What do you think will happen if people see you?"

I could feel Dylan's hand becoming clammy in mine, and I rubbed circles with my thumb to try to calm him down.

"They'll stare, laugh, mock," he spat out, eyes trained on the coffee table. "They'll react just like Flo did."

"What if they react like Eren did?" she pressed on, not minding his lack of eye contact.

"They won't," he told her through clenched teeth. I was sure that Dianne knew what she was doing but I was still worried about Dylan losing his temper with her. I didn't want to interrupt but I didn't want him to lash out at the person who was helping him either.

"I didn't react like Flo," Dianne pointed out.

"Of course you didn't. You're trained not to react to stuff like that," he countered. I was becoming more and more anxious by the second, waiting for my boyfriend to snap at the well-meaning doctor. I opened my mouth to speak but Dianne shocked me by turning to me.

"How do *you* think that people would react to seeing Dylan?"

His face turned to me and I met his gaze. "I don't think it would be as bad as you think. You've healed really well. Yes, there's scarring but it isn't as severe as you think it is," I told him truthfully. "I think if you saw your scar on anyone else you wouldn't think of it as such a big deal."

Dylan continued to stare at me, his eyes conflicted and stormy. It was as if he wanted to believe me but wouldn't let himself. Dianne cleared her throat and we turned our attention back to her.

"Dylan, I'd like to give you something to do from now until the next time I see you." He looked reluctant but gave her a jerky nod. "I know you've been going outside with your hood up and that's great progress. But I'd like you to do it without the hood. I want you to go out in public without hiding yourself." Dylan was already shaking his head before Dianne had finished her sentence and I could feel his hand shaking at the mere thought.

"I can't do that; you know I can't," he fumed. "You're supposed to be helping me, not telling me to do stupid shit that you know will upset me." He jumped from his seat, pulling me with him.

I'd never seen Dylan in a rage like this and I didn't know what to do for the best. Did I let Dianne handle it, or did I step in and try to calm him down? Neither way seemed particularly promising but I opted for the latter. His gaze bounced around the room, not settling on anything for long and avoiding the doctor completely. She seemed to be letting him ride his anger out but I couldn't bring myself to do that. When she looked at him like this, she saw a patient having a moment. When I looked, I saw the man I adored in pain, feeling betrayed by someone he trusted and scared of what they had suggested. I raised myself up onto the tips of my toes and put my hand on his cheek to get his attention. I could only touch the scarred side and I felt him flinch as I made contact.

"Babe, calm down," I pleaded. "Just sit down with me, please."

"No." He shook his head again. "I'm not sitting here and listening to this. Can we please just go?"

I know I should have made him stay but all I wanted to do was make him feel better, so of course, I did as he asked. I mouthed an apology to Dianne as Dylan stomped from the room with his hood firmly in place. In the car, I was about to set off when I caught a flash of Dylan's face as I checked my mirrors. He looked defeated. Tears dripped miserably down his face and each time he attempted to brush them away, more just took their place. I pulled some tissues out of the glove compartment and handed them to him. I could feel the space between my eyebrows puckering from stress and I ground my teeth, waiting for him to give me some kind of signal to either drive away or speak to him. I wasn't sure which one he wanted, and I didn't want to make the wrong guess and make it worse. Eventually, he managed to choke out a request for me to set off and I did so in silence. I rested my hand on his thigh for the drive and his big palm covered it, keeping it in place.

Back at home, Dylan trudged straight upstairs and

I followed him after picking up the post. I found him face down on the bed, and positioned myself beside him, holding the hand-written envelope that had his name on the front. I lay down and dragged my nails over his scalp in the way I knew he liked, and I heard him groan into the pillow.

"Stop being nice to me," he complained. "I don't deserve it."

"I won't stop and you can't make me." I stuck my tongue out, not that he saw it but I hoped he had felt my defiance somehow. "There's something here for you," I told him, placing the envelope in his hand.

He lifted his head to look and dropped it down the side of the bed. "It's from Flo. I don't have the energy to deal with that today, too." He pointed at the offending paper as if it could contaminate him if he held it for too long. I leant over him and grabbed it before putting it away in one of the drawers in the bedside cabinet. "What are you doing?"

"You don't want this now and that's fine," I told him. "But you might tomorrow and I don't want you to lose it."

Chapter Thirty-One

Dylan remained in a sulk for the rest of the day. It would have been irritating if it hadn't been completely heartbreaking. He had been making such progress with Dianne and it was upsetting to see it come to an end so abruptly. I hoped he would schedule another visit but I wasn't stupid enough to hold my breath waiting for it to happen. I was right to keep the letter because Dylan asked for it a few days later. I made myself scarce as he read it, wanting to give him some privacy but he came and found me pretty quickly and insisted that I read it, too.

Dylan,

I'm so sorry. I can't explain how sorry I am.

I acted horribly, to you and to Eren, and I hope you can both forgive me. I had no right to force my presence on you and I was completely in the wrong to bring up Eren's brother like that. I've felt awful ever since.

Please know that I only reacted the way I did when I saw you because I was surprised. There is nothing else to it. I was just shocked to see you. I can see how it came across and that truly was not the case. I was just overwhelmed with the whole situation.

I hope everything is going well for you both and that counselling is helping you. If there's anything I can do to help, please let me know.

I want to explain my actions but don't want to sound as if I'm making excuses for myself. You're my little brother and even though we've always looked out for each other, I've felt a level of responsibility for you since we lost Mum. I know you're an adult and you can take care of yourself but that's just the way I see it. I feel like I'm letting our parents down by not being there with you while you recover, so I pushed you to let me be there for you. It was so wrong of me to disrespect your boundaries that way and I regret it completely.

I hope one day soon we can reconcile things between us and I would love the opportunity to rebuild my friendship with Eren if she can forgive me.

I love you millions,

Flo xxx

I didn't know what to say so I just passed it back to him and continued making our brews.

"What should I do?" he asked, leaning against the counter.

"What do you want to do?"

"I don't know. I do miss her," he pondered. "But..."

"But?"

"I don't know. I feel like there is a *but* but I don't know what the *but* is."

"Then maybe there isn't one," I suggested, handing him his mug and pressing a kiss to his scarred cheek. He flinched, but not as vigorously as he usually did. I took that as a sign of him growing more comfortable.

"So, should I see her?"

"If you want to." I shrugged, nonchalantly.

"What about you? She upset you, too, right?" he reminded me.

I let out a sigh, remembering the ire I'd felt from her thoughtless words. "She did, but that shouldn't matter in terms of you seeing her."

He frowned and it was very clear that he disagreed. "Of course it matters. You're my partner; she shouldn't be upsetting you."

"It's irrelevant anyway. I've calmed down now and I know she didn't say it deliberately to piss me off. Stop trying to use me as an excuse to not decide," I chided him. "I'm not going to tell you what to do, but I will say this. Edward and I used to do our fair share of arguing. We would upset each other, irritate each other, deliberately wind each other up and scream at each other. But we always made up, no matter what we'd been arguing about. I can't imagine how awful I would feel if he'd died and we'd had a rift between us."

I swallowed my feelings, knowing I was being stupid for getting upset over a hypothetical situation but not being able to stop myself. Dylan ran a hand through his hair and closed his eyes.

"I guess I should speak to her. I don't want to see her yet, though."

He called his sister eventually and they had a long conversation. I was working so I wasn't really paying attention, but I heard Dylan saying, "It's okay," a lot so I assumed there were a lot of apologies coming from Flo's side of the discussion. When he hung up, Dylan rested his head on the table and wafted a hand at me. I checked the clock, decided that four thirty was a reasonable finishing time for a Monday, and snapped my laptop shut before going to stand next to him.

"Everything okay?"

"She wouldn't stop saying she was sorry. If anyone else today tells me they're sorry, I'm going to headbutt them," he told me, the delivery deadpan with a face to match. I threw my head back as I laughed, unable to hold it in. *This* was the Dylan I fell in love with. The smart arse, funny, sarcastic Dylan.

"Did you sort things out, though?" I finally asked when I had managed to control myself.

"Yeah, I think so. I've told her she just needs to be patient and that it's not personal."

"Maybe she just needed to hear it from you rather than me," I suggested with a shrug.

"Maybe," he agreed, before turning and running his hands up my thighs.

I cupped his face with both hands and leant down to kiss him. His lips met mine with an enthusiasm I wasn't expecting. It had been a long time since Dylan had had the confidence to instigate anything between us so I was surprised when his hands moved to firmly squeeze my arse. I let out a squeak and he laughed into my mouth, the rumbling sound setting a fire within me. He gripped my hips and pulled me so that I was sitting on him, my legs spread over his. I moved easily, letting him guide me and touch me to his heart's content.

It was an amazing feeling, having him take control, and it reminded me of how much he'd wanted me when we first started seeing each other. His face was buried in my chest, kissing the soft skin there as his hands crawled up my legs to the spot I needed him most.

I rolled my hips, hoping for some relief but getting none. I was only wearing a tank top and shorts, so that flimsy material was barely a barrier between us. The problem was that my legs were wide open with nothing between them. I let out a mewl of complaint as one of his hands moved to palm my breast and the other teased around the edge of the shorts. Again I rolled my hips in the hopes that I could tease his hand up to my core but I had no such luck. Dylan figured out what I was doing immediately and he let me know it by giving me a sharp spank on the exposed skin on my leg. I jumped, not expecting it but thoroughly enjoying it. It didn't hurt properly but the tingle it left combined with the sound had me even more frustrated and I needed more.

He rubbed the sting away with his warm palm and his fingers brushed up my shorts. I felt his finger hook but it was met with nothing but skin.

"Are you not wearing underwear?" he asked, his eyes gleaming. I bit my lip and shook my head, enjoying his shocked features.

He leant into me until his cheek was against mine and his teeth grazed my ear as he whispered, "You have *no* idea how much that turns me on."

I pushed my chest up against his, the fabric rubbing over my hardened nipples making me shudder. "Show me."

He grabbed my hand from his shoulder and pressed it down to his crotch. I felt his erection twitch in his pants and squirmed in his lap, itching to make him as pent up and frustrated as I was. But I behaved and let him take the lead, not wanting to do anything to knock his confidence.

He grabbed the front of my vest and tore it open, shredding the fabric like wet tissue paper. The movement was violent but the passion behind it left me in awe. His head dipped and he took my nipple between his teeth while he pinched the other one. His free hand was still on mine, and he moved to hold it over his heart. My head fell back and I lavished in the attention he was giving me. I could feel his heart pounding rapidly in his ribcage and I was sure the rhythm of my own matched it.

His hand left my breast and grazed down my stomach until it hit the waistband of my shorts. His fingers dipped underneath and my breath caught in my throat. I whined, egging him on to give me what I needed. He teased me, brushing his fingers over my clit until, without warning, he slid a digit inside me and I cried out at the invasion. His other hand left mine and gripped the back of my neck, moving my head forward to look at him.

"You're so fucking wet," he forced through clenched teeth, trying to hold himself back. I could hear the moisture as he slid a second finger into me, and I would have been embarrassed if it had been anyone else who had got me into such a state. "Tell me you want me," he demanded, his thumb swiping over my clit and sending a shockwave of pleasure through me.

"I want you, Dylan. I want you so fucking much,"

I moaned, barely able to hold myself up as he continued to explore me. All too soon, his fingers left me and my hips moved to chase them, not ready for the moment to end. My eyes widened as he lifted his fingers to his mouth and sucked them. Knowing where they'd been made my core clench, and when he kissed me, I could taste myself on his tongue.

"Take me to bed?" I begged him shamelessly.

The neediness in my voice must have been a turn on because he lifted me from his lap and stood up without my feet ever touching the floor. He strode across the room and up the stairs. The strength he exhibited carrying me all that way turned me on like you wouldn't believe, and I nipped at his neck the whole way, leaving little red marks as evidence of my presence.

He dropped me onto the bed, falling forwards so he was hovering over me. I took advantage of his t-shirt hanging off his stomach to tug it over his head, revealing his washboard abs. I dragged my finger down them and he shuddered. I used one hand to push him up so I could shuffle back up the bed, but when he lifted his head up, he stopped moving all together. I followed his line of sight and realised why he'd stopped.

The mirror.

Stupid, stupid Eren.

I'd forgotten it was there and Dylan was transfixed. His expression had morphed into one of horror as he saw himself hovering over me. He looked back down at me and I saw the walls going up in his eyes. I scrambled, desperate to put a stop to this reaction that was about to ruin everything. He was already moving away from me, pushing himself to stand. I went with him, kneeling up on the bed so that I was as close to his height as possible.

"Dylan, stop it. Come back to me." I pulled him into me, pressing my lips to his to try to incite some reaction, but all I got were his hands on my hips, trying to stop me.

"Eren, you don't have to-"

"But I want to," I whispered, undoing his jeans and pushing them down to his ankles. I rubbed his cock through his boxers and couldn't help licking my lips.

"Jesus, Eren," he hissed, his eyes scrunched closed as if he were desperate not to catch sight of us in the mirror again.

He tipped his head down and opened them again to look at me. His confidence had wavered but he was too horny to want to stop what was happening. His hand drifted downwards and stroked between my folds.

"Still so wet," he hummed.

I pulled his cock free and kept one hand moving on it while the other went to his jaw and pushed it up, giving me access to his throat. I kissed up the column of his neck and nipped his ear lobe, making him jump.

When I was sure he was fully into what was happening, I pulled his hand away from me and turned so my back was to him. I bent over and placed myself so his cock was centimetres from my entrance. I leant back onto him and heard him groan as my muscles clenched around him. His hands drifted to my hips and held with enough force to leave bruises. I rocked away again, trying to torment him into taking charge again and it worked. He dragged me backwards, thrusting his hips at the same time and ramming himself into me. I cried out, loving the feeling of him stretching me out. He held still when he was fully inside me and I felt his lips press between my shoulder blades. I consciously flexed my muscles, encouraging him to move.

He traced kisses down my spine as he worked up a pace that felt incredible for the both of us. When he was fully straightened back up, I took a peek in the mirror and watched him take me from behind. It was hands down the hottest thing I'd ever seen and I wanted him to see it too.

I lifted myself up so my back was against his chest whilst keeping him inside of me. He had one hand on my clit, circling it lazily, and the other hand was around my neck, moving it to the side so he could sink his teeth into the tender skin just below my ear. We looked phenomenal, and what I saw in the mirror was something I wanted to look at forever.

I felt him speed up and knew he was close to the edge. I took advantage of the moment, knowing that nothing could stop either of us at that point.

"Dylan," I panted. "Dylan, open your eyes." His face didn't change in the mirror. I lifted my hand to the one around my throat and squeezed his wrist. "Please, I want you to look at me when you cum."

They were the magic words that brought us to the crescendo. His eyes met mine in the glass and I saw his face change as he saw how we looked. When we let ourselves go, it was mind blowing. Seeing each other's reactions was incredible. I felt all of my muscles relax but he held me up against him, still staring into the mirror. He let go of my neck, and his arms went around my waist and hugged me to him. He brushed the hair from my face and rested his chin on my shoulder. I turned to kiss him and he met me there before looking back to the mirror.

"Thank you." His voice was breathless and full of emotion.

"What for?"

"Showing me us."

Chapter Thirty-Two

Our tryst in front of the mirror did wonders for Dylan's confidence. Seeing what he did to me helped him accept what I'd been telling him for so long. He couldn't argue and say that I found him unappealing when the obvious truth was in his face like that. Even when we weren't having sex, he liked to pull me in front of it and watch my face as I looked at our reflection.

"On my own, I still hate how I look," he explained.

"But the way you look at us together, you make it feel right. Like there's nothing wrong with me."

"There *is* nothing wrong with you," I told him for the millionth time. "But even you have to admit, we just look right together."

I could see the wheels turning in his mind, trying to come up with an argument until a smile formed on his rosy lips. "We do. It shouldn't make sense but I can't picture either of us any other way."

Dylan's confidence boost didn't only extend to me. He finally agreed to see his sister and I found myself tearing up at their reunion. Flo was sheepish when she entered and Dylan was nervous. He had been pacing around the kitchen for an hour before she arrived and I could feel myself going dizzy just watching him.

They kept their distance from each other at first, neither one wanting to overwhelm the other. It was like watching two nervous cats bumping into each other in the street. I disappeared from the room with the intention of making everyone something to drink but after less than a minute, I could hear Dylan's footsteps behind me.

"What's up, babe?" I asked, dumping tea bags into the bin. I saw his shadow loom over me and felt his warmth on my back. I turned to face him and he caught me in his arms.

"You left," he said.

"Yeah, I thought a drink might make you both feel a little more comfortable," I explained, holding up the mugs in defence, not wanting him to think I'd just abandoned him.

"Thank you, but I need you with me. I can't do this on my own, not yet." I smiled up at him, grateful for his honesty.

"Well if you grab me the milk, we can go back in."

I handed Flo her tea, and Dylan sat in Edward's arm chair, pulling me to sit on his lap so that I acted as a buffer between them. I'd seen him do something similar to this before in the doctor's office when he tried to hide behind me to avoid letting Dianne see his face. I readjusted so that I was sitting across him with my legs dangling over the arm of the chair. I felt Dylan stiffen beneath me and we both assessed Flo's face to see if there was any discernible reaction there. I smiled when she didn't so much as blink, and leant my head onto Dylan's shoulder, letting my fingers drift along his forearm. As with Dianne, I didn't say much, letting the two of them lead the conversation and being there to support my boyfriend if he needed me. It was far more enjoyable with the siblings, though. They reminded me of happy memories with Edward with their inside jokes and shared memories. It was nice to see Dylan warming back up to her and letting her in. I was so proud of him for coming this far in such a short space of time. By the time Flo left, there was a feeling of warmth in the atmosphere and even I felt my spirits lift just seeing the two of them smiling at each other. She caught me just before she left and pulled me to one side when Dylan went to take our mugs back to the kitchen.

"Eren, I just wanted to tell you that I'm really sorry for what I said. I had no business bringing Edward into things and if I could take back that entire day, I would."

I pulled her into a hug and squeezed her tight. She sagged into me and I heard her sigh of relief as she hugged me back. "Don't worry about it. We're good."

Once she was gone, we were both exhausted so we ordered a take away and slonked around in our pyjamas for the rest of the evening. Iggy was happy not going out. He'd spent so much time running around and jumping on furniture with excitement at seeing Flo again that the poor pup had exhausted himself and had tapped out on Edward's chair for the night. Dylan and I sat at the table, picking at Chinese food and talking about what we were going to do with our weekend.

"I feel like we should go somewhere," Dylan mused. "I've been a terrible boyfriend lately." I didn't like that so, naturally, I threw a vegetable spring roll at him.

"You have not, now behave yourself," I chastised, trying not to laugh as the spring roll bounced off his head and onto the floor.

"Wow, Eren, how rude." He snorted, picking up the delicious missile. "Still, I think we should do something."

"What did you have in mind?"

"I don't know. Maybe we could go to the Lake District or something. Iggy could run around to his heart's content, and we could pack a picnic and walk up some hills."

"It'll be cold," I warned him.

"We've got coats; we'll be fine," he assured me, but I wasn't convinced.

"Maybe we should wait and see what the weather's like. If Iggy gets too muddy he'll blend in with the dirt and we might never find him again." I chuckled.

"That is true. If it's raining, we'll do something else. I just thought it might be nice to go out and that's the kind of thing where we're less likely to bump into other people," he explained, frowning ever so slightly.

"It's a great idea. I love it. I just don't want the three of us to flood the car coming home, that's all." I blew him a kiss across the table before scoffing a mouthful of fried rice in a very unladylike manner.

Our night was spent under blankets on the sofa, watching cheesy superhero flicks and playing chess on my tablet. I used to think I was good at chess until I started playing with Dylan. It was effortless for him; his mind had a natural flare for strategy games. He was always three moves ahead of me and out of five games, I didn't win once. He teased me as I tried to be smart and plan out moves that he easily blocked or countered, and the longer it went on, the worse I got. Eventually, I got to the point where I forfeited, begrudgingly announcing his reign as Chess King of the House.

Chapter Thirty-Three

Flo became a weekly visitor in our home, and I was pleased that Dylan had someone other than myself that he could lean on. Of course I was still there for him as much as he needed, but it did him some good to have someone outside of our relationship. His boss had also been in contact recently to ask when, if ever, he planned to go back to work.

"I don't know what to tell him."

"Well, what are your plans?" I asked.

"I don't know."

"So tell him that then."

"He can't keep my job open forever with me on sick leave. Eventually, he's going to have to fill the position whether it's with me or someone else. I have enough savings to keep me going for a while but it won't last forever."

I had been thinking about his work situation myself for a while and had worked out that if I took on some private clients outside of work hours, I could support the both of us indefinitely. I hadn't said anything because he hadn't, but it felt like it was as good a time as any to tell him.

"You know, you don't have to go back," I hinted. He looked at me like I was mad.

"Of course I do. How else am I going to pay bills?"

"Well, I kept the house paid up on my own before you moved in. I can do it again. If I take on a private client here and there, I can support the two of us until you find something else you want to do." He gaped at me like he couldn't believe what I was saying. "I have some pretty reasonable savings put aside so you wouldn't need to dip into yours once your sick pay cuts off," I carried on, not wanting to sit in the awkward silence.

"So what, I'll just be a house husband?"

"If you want." I shrugged. "I'm not saying you

shouldn't go back. I'm just saying you don't *have* to go back. It's just an option."

An array of emotions crossed his features: apprehension, anxiety, affection, guilt. The last one confused me until he spoke again.

"You shouldn't have to pay my way for me. That's not what you signed on for when we got together."

I sighed, knowing that I should have expected this response. I turned on the couch to face him.

"I wouldn't be *paying your way*. I'd just be helping you out, and even if you decided you weren't going back to work ever, I wouldn't mind."

"I will go back eventually," he said, his eyes sincere. "Just not yet."

"Will you go back to the construction site?" I asked. I didn't want to show it but the thought of him being back in the place where he'd been hurt put me on edge. Of course, if he *did* want to, I would support him, but if it was up to me I would rather he didn't.

"I'd rather not, if I can avoid it. But if I quit, who knows how long I'll be unemployed for?"

"That's not important. Ignore that bit for now. Right this second, do you want to go back to work there, or not?"

"No."

I smiled encouragingly. "Then tell your boss that and we'll go from there."

Dylan sent his boss an email with his letter of resignation attached and received one back with well wishes and a promise that if he re-considered and wanted to go back at a later date, there would be no hard feelings if his application were to end up on the boss' desk. It seemed like a weight had been lifted off his shoulders and it felt good to know that I'd helped make that pressure go away.

I wasn't stupid; I knew at some point he would probably want to go back to work and feel independent again, but I had meant it when I said there was no time frame. All I cared about was him getting to a place where he felt confident enough to go out and work if that was what he wanted.

For the time being, he was content running the house and he did an excellent job. Personally, I'd only even seen it so clean when I had gone away for the weekend and Edward had deep cleaned while I wasn't there to mess it up. I was hopeful that this would be another step on his journey to living the way he used to.

Chapter Thirty-Four

I dreamt that we were in a distant place, somewhere hot and bright. The sand was soft, almost white under our feet. We walked along it barefooted, enjoying the heat that it held. The sea was the perfect blue that you only see in movies, and I was in awe when I looked out to the horizon. Gentle waves lapped at the shore. The sound soothed every frayed nerve I had and I felt like I could inhale properly for the first time in forever. It was like the sea air was cleansing my body of everything awful that had happened in the last eighteen months and left room for only the good. I pulled Dylan down the sand to the sea, wanting to feel the water washing over my toes. He came with me, willing to submit to my every whim and fancy.

Everything about us physically was the same but the aura was different. I felt carefree, uninhibited, lighter than air. I looked up at Dream Dylan and he smiled down at me with an expression that held nothing but pure love and adoration. It was just the two of us and therefore he had no need to be anxious. I think that was the biggest difference of all.

When I woke up, I felt the weight of reality pressing down on me. With a sigh, I rolled over and reached out to Dylan's side of the bed. My fingers itched to feel him and I hummed in contentment when I found him. I expected him to respond in a similar way but I felt tension radiating from him.

"Babe, are you okay?" I asked, shuffling myself closer to him. He didn't say anything; he just shrugged and handed me his phone.

Flo: Dad's here. He wants to see you.

"But, that's good, isn't it?"

"I haven't told him what happened," Dylan confessed, looking at his hands.

"Why not?"

"Because of what he used to say to me as a kid." He shook his head slightly, and while I wanted to know what on earth was happening, I waited for him to gather himself. "I haven't told you much about my dad because I didn't imagine you'd ever meet him. When he moved away, it was a relief. Flo was always close to him but I wasn't. Dad was successful because he was smart and he worked his way up to a big time position in the company he worked for." He took a deep breath and started picking at his hands. I tangled my fingers with his, and he squeezed my hands but didn't look up. "Flo was always clever but I wasn't. I'm still not." I opened my mouth to argue but he didn't give me a chance to get a word in. "He would always tell me that the best I could hope for was a shitty job and a wife who overlooked my stupidity. While Flo was told she could be anything she wanted, I was taught that my face was the only thing I had going for me and even then, that was pushing it."

I'd had no idea that Dylan had grown up this way. Suddenly, his insecurities made more sense and my heart cracked in two.

"Now that this has happened, he'll have all the more reason to put me down."

"No, he'll have nothing because you're in a good place."

He shook his head, finally looking at me but smiling sadly. "I'm exactly what he always said I would be—an unemployed loser, living off his girlfriend."

"Don't say that; you know it isn't true. Don't let him get to you before he's even here."

"I can't help it. He lives, rent free, in my head and I can't get him out. He's buried right in there and he'll get to you too."

"Dylan, you aren't making sense. I would never think that of you. You know that." My morning had gone from calm and relaxed to tense and upsetting in a flash. I hated hearing him talk about himself this way. I saw his eyes growing pink and watery, although he tried to hide it from me, dropping my hand and scrubbing it over his face.

"You don't right now, but you will. He'll show you all the things that make me worthless and you'll realise that I'm a waste of your time." His full lips trembled and his eyebrows furrowed as he tried to hold in his emotions. I could see all of the progress he'd made slipping away from him *again*. He was fighting to stop it but it was like he was trying to cling on to mist. I moved to put my hands onto his face and he flinched away from my touch.

That flinch snapped something within me and I was furious at this man I'd never even met. I hated that he held enough power over Dylan to undo all of his work. I felt my spine stiffen and my resolve set itself in stone. I flung my leg over his so I was straddling him, and forced him to look at me. The tear stains on his cheeks softened my expression and I wiped them away. He flinched again at my touch but I ignored the response.

"After everything we've been through, do you really think that one bitter old man can change my feelings for you?"

"You don't know him-"

"I don't need to. I know *you* and that is enough for me to know that nothing your dad has to say can make a difference to me."

"You can't be sure of that," he whispered, his voice cracking. I swallowed the lump that was in my throat and my eyes stung. I could feel him retreating into himself and I was desperate to stop him.

"I understand it's hard to let go of things that are ingrained into you for years, but just because he says it doesn't mean it's true." I could see in his face that he wasn't convinced, so I changed tactics. "Is there anything anyone could say about me that would make you leave me?"

His eyes widened in shock and his hands flew to my face. "No, of course not. You're everything to me."

I couldn't help smiling at that and nestled my head into his hands.

"So why wouldn't I be the same way? I love you so much, Dylan. Nothing—*nothing*—is going to get in the way of that. Can you please just trust me on this?"

I leant in to kiss him. He was still tense at first but when I nipped his bottom lip, he pulled me into him. His kisses were usually sweet, passionate and loving, but this one was different. It was scared, desperate, and panicked.

"Promise me you'll still be here, no matter what he says?" Dylan begged, his hands clamped around my waist as if to hold me in place.

"I promise, but you know you don't have to see him if you don't want to."

"If I don't he'll just harass Flo until I do."

"What does Flo think about the way your dad treats you?" I asked, curious.

"She doesn't know the extent of it, I never wanted it to tarnish her relationship with him. She knows we don't get on but when we were kids I really tried to shield her from that side of him."

I stroked my fingertips down his face as my heart swelled in my chest. This man was so compassionate. It would've been so easy for him to resent his sister but instead he tried to protect her. It made me love him even more.

Once again, Dylan was pacing, but this time he was waiting for a visit from his dad. Flo was working, as Dylan had hoped, and it was just going to be the two of them, plus me. I tried to get him to sit down but he couldn't keep still, needing to occupy himself in order to prevent a total meltdown. When we heard the knock on the door, Dylan froze and I saw his hands shaking.

"Babe, why don't you go and get the tea and coffee pots and I'll let your dad in," I suggested, thinking it was best to give him some time to gather himself. I thought wrong, though, and he shook his head vehemently.

"No, I need to be with you. I know I'm being clingy and I'm sorry about it, but you keep me grounded," he explained, his eyes flitting between me and the hallway. Another knock thumped out and Dylan flinched. "I should let him in," he mumbled.

I tried to guide him to the door but his feet wouldn't budge. I wrapped one of my arms around his waist, putting one hand up the back of his shirt. I gently dragged my nails against his skin, trying to bring him back to me. He met my gaze with tight eyes and a locked jaw.

"It'll be fine, I promise."

"Don't leave me."

"I won't."

We went to the door together and I gave Dylan's hand one last squeeze before opening it. The man on the other side was not what I expected. Des Turner was shorter than I was and incredibly frail. His skin had taken on that leather handbag quality that came with ageing in the sun. His face was lined and his jowls quivered as the old man's watery brown eyes took in his son.

"What the hell happened to you?"

Dylan opened his mouth and closed it again, looking at his feet. I could see that he wasn't going to be saying anything anytime soon so I took over.

"Would you like to come in?"

The elderly man grunted at me and pushed past his son. I closed the door behind him and directed him to the living room. I pulled Dylan to Edward's arm chair and he shot me a grateful look. Once he had sat down, I perched myself on the arm of the chair, wanting to be nearby to shield him from anything his father had to say.

"So," the man said gruffly. "Who are you?" He narrowed his eyes at me.

"I'm Eren, Dylan's girlfriend."

"Never heard of you," he rumbled dismissively. "What did you do to end up like that?" He tilted his chin to his son.

"Gas explosion," Dylan mumbled. "Workplace accident." I saw him try to turn his face away to hide his scars.

"Well," his dad chuckled, "I guess you won't be able to rely on your face anymore. What are you gonna do now?"

"I don't know."

"Speak up, boy!" he barked across the room, making both Dylan and Iggy jump.

"I said, I don't know."

I hated the shame that was evident in his voice. How could a parent be so callous about their child's health? I was furious but I held my tongue. Dylan didn't need me to argue with his dad; he just needed my support.

"You know, I'm not surprised something like this happened," the old man mused. "You always were stupid enough to get into a serious accident. If anything, it's a miracle it's only happened now."

Dylan flinched at the barbs his father threw at him but the old man didn't let it stop him.

"I suppose you must at least be getting a nice payout. Why else would *she* be arsed with you?" Dylan shook his head, his auburn hair quivering around his face. His father let out a laugh that chilled the blood in my veins. "You're fucked then; she'll never stay." His almost empty eyes sparkled with malice and I felt Dylan's grip on my thigh tighten, almost to the point of pain. I lifted his hand off me and slid from the arm of the chair so I was on his lap. I felt some of the tension leave him but his arms were still like steel around me. I was torn between comforting him and letting him deal with his father's bullshit in his own way.

My self control very nearly snapped but I heard his voice from behind me and I beamed with pride.

"She will." It was quiet and hoarse as his voice threatened to abandon him, but he'd said it. He'd stood up to the vicious old man who had spent so long putting him down.

"And what are you going to offer her to make her stay?" Des challenged, enjoying his son's discomfort.

"I- I-" Dylan tried to respond but nothing came out. His arms shook around me and I could hear him swallowing thickly.

"You really don't know him at all do you?" I had finally reached the end of my tether and I couldn't hold back any longer. It killed me to watch Dylan get walked all over, and as much as I wanted him to stick up for himself, I couldn't push down the urge to defend him. "Dylan and I were together before the accident and nothing has changed. You might not see it, but your son is an incredible man. He is kind and loving and considerate." I took a heaving breath, letting the anger drop from my tone. "Somehow, despite your poison, Dylan has ended up as an exceptional person. Nothing that you say can *ever* negate that. Now please, get out of our house."

Chapter Thirty-Five

Des didn't need to be asked twice, but he couldn't resist one last spew of venom at my boyfriend.

"You'll never keep her looking like that. You're going to be ugly and alone."

I slammed the door on him, not wanting to let him taint our perfectly good air any longer. "Fucking guy," I huffed under my breath.

After flicking the latch, I immediately pulled

Dylan flush towards me with my back against the door. We'd been in a similar situation before but this time there was nothing sexual about it. This was all about comfort and reassurance. He sagged against me and let out a heavy exhale. I let my hand drift to the bottom of his back and gently stroked his skin. I felt his form shudder against me and I knew he was trying to hide from me the fact that he was crying. In a way, I was glad. I hoped his tears would purge all of the badness left behind by his father's presence. But I didn't want him to cover it up. I pushed him off me and held his face between my palms.

"I'm proud of you," I whispered, kissing away the moisture on his cheeks. He tried to shake his head but I held him in place, forcing him to keep looking at me. "Tell me what you're thinking."

"He's right. I can't offer you anything." His voice cracked on the last word and my heart did the same. I pushed myself up onto my toes and pressed my lips to his.

"We don't *offer* each other anything. This isn't a business transaction." Rolling back onto my heels I tugged at his hands, pulling us until we were back on the armchair with me on his lap. "I'm not with you because of what you can give me. I'm with you because you make me happy." He didn't argue; he just looked at me with sad eyes, framed by wet lashes. "After I lost Edward, I didn't think I would ever be able to enjoy life again. I was able to exist comfortably but I didn't feel surges of joy about things like I had beforehand. But then I met you, and things felt fun again. It was like you lit up every part of me you touched and I could breathe again. There wasn't a dark hue over everything anymore."

"And then this happened and fucked it." He threw an accusatory hand to his face and I caught his hand, lacing our fingers together and caressing his injured cheek with our knuckles.

"No, this happened and nothing changed between us. We still love each other, we still want each other." I leant in and touched my forehead to his. "You know I'm right. This is just *him* messing with your head. He doesn't know what he's talking about so don't pay him any mind."

We stayed there for a long time after Dylan's dad had gone. He seemed to take in what I had said and relaxed underneath me but his hold on me was still firm, as if I might make a run for it at any moment.

The evening rolled around and Flo sent me a message.

Flo: I've got a class tonight. Do you two fancy it?

I turned my phone to Dylan, showing him the message and he shook his head immediately.

"Not today. After everything with Dad, I just want to spend the night with you. I just... I don't know. I just feel like I need to hold you, you know?" He stuttered, flexing his arms around me to accentuate his point. I smiled at him and nodded as I quickly typed out a message back.

Eren: Not today. I'll try and bring him along next week.

I threw my phone onto the couch and received a glare from Iggy for daring to interrupt his sleep. His mood didn't last, though, as he yawned, showing off his tiny teeth before walking around in a circle on the cushion and going straight back to sleep. I really envied dogs and their ability to sleep at any given moment. I rested my head on Dylan's shoulder, my face buried into the crook of his neck, and relaxed, moulding my body to fit the contours of his. As if he couldn't get me close enough, he slumped further down into the seat, pulling me with him and cradling me in his arms. I was so comfortable, so content, that it was easy to imagine we were in our own little bubble. Untouchable and unwavering.

Chapter Thirty-Six

The visit from Des set Dylan back slightly, but it could have been worse. His confidence was shaken, but only in terms of our relationship. I was pleased to see that he was continuing to get back to his old self when it came to the general public.

He had started small, driving me to and from work, nipping out to the corner shop with me, just little bits and pieces. But I decided to take the plunge and suggest we do something a bit more social. I had made steak and chips for tea in the hopes that it would butter him up, and I waited until he was full and smiling before making my case. He knew immediately that I was sucking up to him and I could tell from the glint in his eye that he was enjoying the extra attention, not that he was ever starved of it anyway. I was lying with my head in his lap on the couch, gazing up at his strong jawline when I decided to bite the bullet and go for it.

"Do you fancy going to yoga tomorrow when I finish work?"

He looked down at me and I watched his expression, ready to jump up and placate him at any moment in case my request set off a round of panic. He just looked at me with a gentle smile and nodded his head.

"I think I'd enjoy that."

I shot up into a sitting position, nearly cracking my head off his chin on the way. "Really?"

"It would make you happy, right?"

I nodded. "But don't do it just for that. I don't want you stressing just for me."

"No, I think it'll be good. I need to go out and see other humans at some point."

I was ecstatic at how easily he had agreed and I did a little happy dance in my seat as he messaged his sister to let her know we would be coming.

I'd specifically suggested yoga on Wednesday because, according to Flo, it was usually the quietest night. I didn't want to risk him becoming overwhelmed with too many people around. This way, he didn't need to be too close to anyone and we could hide out at the back and do our own thing. I secretly hoped he would get back into helping Flo teach the classes but he wasn't ready for that yet.

I really wanted the session to go well. In my head, I'd come to the conclusion that if he could do this, it would open the gate for him to do everything else he had done previously. I could tell he missed the social aspects of his old life, and there was only so much cleaning you could do in one house before you started to get bored. I had noticed him becoming cabin feverish and while I encouraged him to get out and do things, I knew it was still hard for him, especially on his own. He'd gone out with Flo for a coffee once, and his old boss had been to the house to see how he was doing, but it wasn't enough. He needed more.

Chapter Thirty-Seven

The car park was fairly empty when we arrived at the yoga centre and I let out a tiny sigh of relief. We'd brought Iggy with us and he was very excited to be back at his old haunt, bounding in way ahead of us. The hallway rang with laughter as we entered, no doubt due to my dog's shenanigans, but it made Dylan freeze beside me. His hand on mine became a vice and I turned to look at him. His face was a mask of pain and my eyes flew around the room, looking for anything that might have triggered him.

"What is it, babe?"

"They're laughing at me," he croaked, his chin dipped towards his chest. I realised that he'd put two and two together and made eighteen.

"No, they're not. Why would anyone be laughing at you?"

"I think we all know why."

"How could they be? We haven't even seen anyone yet!" I knew it was just his own insecurities preying on him but I had no idea how to convince *him* of that. "Please, just come in with me and you'll see that you're wrong." I was interrupted by Iggy's yapping as he realised we hadn't followed him into the room. "I swear, if you still don't feel right we can leave but please, just give me a chance to show you that everything's okay." My eyes were beseeching him to give it a chance and after I pulled him into me for a hug, he exhaled heavily into my hair, took in an equally heavy breath, and turned to face the double doors, his head held high.

I pushed the doors open gently, and rather than going to chat with everyone like I usually would have, I stayed with Dylan at the back of the hall to set up our mats a safe distance from the rest of the group.

The telltale sound of Iggy's paws against the hardwood floor made me turn around, and I saw one of Flo's regulars following him. I was ashamed to say that in my head, I'd called her Leopard Lady since I'd first met her, due to the animal print leggings she wore for most of the sessions. I threw her a smile but she wasn't looking at me. Her eyes were focused on Dylan and she looked torn between excited and furious.

"Dylan, where the hell have you been?" I stiffened, as did he, and I moved closer to him, acting as a buffer between the two of them. Dylan looked at me, his eyes wide in panic and a storm brewing in his irises. I sent up a silent prayer that he wouldn't snap at this poor wisp of a woman who had no idea what she was walking into, and I remained tense as Dylan turned around to face her. The woman's jaw dropped and I was ready to step in until she spoke again, in a voice that was affectionate and sympathetic.

"Oh honey, I'm so sorry. I had no idea. I didn't mean to be insensitive."

I grazed my nails over the back of his hand and waited for his reply. I quite literally sagged with relief when he finally gave her a response. "Don't worry about it, Rhonda. It's not exactly common knowledge."

"We just thought you were too loved up with this

one to join us." Her voice wobbled, still worried that she'd offended him with her goofy joke, and she flashed an apologetic glance my way. I gave her a meagre smile, still concerned about my man but not wanting her to worry that she'd upset me too.

"It's fine," he assured her, polite but obviously irked. "You couldn't have known." I was grateful that Rhonda realised this was a good time to leave us be, and she reached out to pat him on the arm.

"It's good to see you again, dear."

Dylan sat down on his mat after she'd walked away and his head drooped between his shoulders. I placed myself in the same position, facing him, and rubbed my hands on his thighs.

"Are you okay?" Instead of answering, he grabbed my hand and placed it on his chest. I could feel his heart thudding against his sternum and I used my knuckles to lift his chin. "Do you want to leave?"

"I don't know," he whispered. His usually velvet voice was full of gravel and sand. "I know it's weird because we're in public, but could you please come here?" He opened his arms to me and I knocked his legs open so I could get in between them. On my knees with my arms around his neck and my chin resting on his shoulder, I felt one arm go around my waist and the other around my shoulders. He buried his face in my neck and his hot breath made my skin erupt into goosebumps. I stroked down his back in the hopes of soothing him and I heard him gently hum as I did. In our own little world, Dylan relaxed enough to stay and Flo called the class to attention so that we could start.

By the time we got home, Dylan seemed fine, albeit exhausted. We hadn't hung around for a chat at the end like we'd used to but we got a couple of minutes with Flo in the car park. She was obviously thrilled that Dylan had come back to her classes and I was sure her cheeks must have ached from her blinding smile.

We showered together and I used the time to massage his muscles, easing out the knots in his shoulders and rubbing away as much tension as I could. Sounds of appreciation rumbled deep in his chest. I wished we could live in that moment forever. We were closed off in our own little bubble of peace and quiet. Nothing could touch us there and we were safe; he was safe with me.

Chapter Thirty-Eight

"So, how's it going with lover boy?" Angela teased, eyeing me over her cappuccino.

"It's great. He's come so far," I told her, pride lighting my eyes. Dylan had gone from being anxious to leave the house with me, to volunteering to help Flo teach again after a few weeks of practice.

The visit from his Dad had shaken him but he'd come through it and we were stronger than ever. He had finally come to terms with what had happened to him and had accepted that I was staying by his side, for better or worse, in sickness and in health.

There was more that I needed to tell Angela and I was buzzing with excitement, but I also had to wait for Layla and predictably, she was late. We were about to order a second coffee when she appeared, flustered and red in the face.

"I'm sorry, I'm sorry, I'm sorry," she gasped, collapsing into the metal chair with a clang. "I got held up with a client who just would not shut up." We laughed at her and ordered more coffees. Once they arrived, the girls looked at me, expectant and impatient.

"So," I started, thrilled to finally say this out loud. "I need a favour this weekend." They both nodded, expressions wary and confused. "Dylan and I are eloping and I want you to be my bridesmaids."

"Oh my God."

"You're what?"

"Oh my God."

"Eren, that's amazing, congratulations," Angela gushed, while Layla continued to repeat the same shocked sentence. I giggled into my mug at my best friend's response.

"So will you come with us?" I checked, fairly certain that the answer would be yes.

"Of course I will."

"Fuck yeah, I will." Layla all but shouted. "I want to see my bestie get married!"

There was a lot of squealing around our table and I felt filled with warmth and love. I was so grateful that I could count on my girls to support my decision. I'd been worried they would think me selfish for wanting to run away and do this in private but neither Dylan nor myself were the kind of people who wanted a big spectacle. All we needed was each other, Layla, Angela and our small families. Actually, I also needed a dress. Nothing huge but it just felt like getting married in pyjamas was a step too far really. We arranged to go dress hunting later in the week and spent the rest of our coffee meeting discussing the logistics of getting us all to the registry office. I had four weeks to plan my mini wedding and I was confident that with the team I'd built, it'd be a piece of cake.

I would like to retract my previous *piece of cake* comment because I was stupid and it was not, in fact, a piece of cake. Why was it so hard to get flowers? They grew out of the ground, for Christ's sake. In the end, I settled for some fake ones and called it a day. At least no one would be affected by hayfever.

Dress shopping for the girls was surprisingly easy—knee-length tea dresses in pale pink with suede high heels that matched. I was the hardest to buy for because I was so fussy. I wanted something that was bridal but not like, *bridal*, you know? I ended up in the same style as my bridesmaids but in white with long sleeves and an underskirt to give it some volume. My shoes were lacy, too, and I jazzed the ensemble up with sparkly jewellery and a half length veil.

It might not have sounded like much to some people but when I put the whole outfit together, I felt beautiful. The underskirt made me feel like I was about to go and perform Swan Lake at Covent Garden. I was too busy twirling around in said dress to realise that the front door had opened and closed until I heard Dylan right outside the bedroom talking to Iggy.

"Don't come in," I called, panicking.

"Babe, are you okay?" he asked, his voice marred with anxiety.

"I'm fine. I'm just in my dress," I told him through the thin wood separating us. "I'll be out in a minute."

I heard him chuckle and his footsteps grew quieter

as he wandered back downstairs. There wasn't going to be much that was traditional about our wedding but I wanted the dress to stay a surprise.

When I'd finally gotten out of the garment, I took the stairs two at a time and practically fell right into Dylan's open arms.

"Promise you'll catch me like that tomorrow if I fall down the aisle," I joked, loving the way he held me so effortlessly.

"Of course I would, but maybe do your best to stay upright anyway?"

We were both so excited we could barely eat. Knowing that in twenty-four hours we would be man and wife was an incredible feeling. I wanted nothing more than to be tied to the man next me in every way possible. At that point, it felt more like a need than anything else. I couldn't imagine an existence without him.

In bed that night, I climbed on top of him, kissing him deeply and exploring him with reckless abandon.

"Hey, this is going be your last time having sex as an unmarried woman," Dylan pointed out with a smirk. "You sure you want to waste that occasion on me?"

I rolled my eyes at him and kissed my way down his

chest, nipping every now and again as I went. When I got to his waistband, I stopped and looked up at him through my lashes.

"I'm very, very sure."

Chapter Thirty-Nine

Dylan

I had left early in the morning, going to get ready at Flo's so we could meet my girl at the registry office. I had been reluctant to leave, part of me expecting to be left waiting at the altar. Actually, no, not expecting it, just thinking I would deserve it. I knew Eren would never actually do that to me. It was just my brain, wired to think the worst things about myself.

It was unreal how much she'd helped me with that.

Her unending love and support were far more than I deserved yet she never let up. It would have been so easy for her to walk away and write me off as a bad decision. In fact, at times I had actively encouraged her to do so. But I couldn't deny the relief I felt every time she shot down my suggestion and stayed by my side. I would spend the rest of my days trying to make her feel as loved as she made me feel. I was thinking about exactly that over breakfast with my sister when she rudely interrupted me.

"So, remind me again why you're eloping instead of having a normal wedding?"

"Didn't want one," I told her, my mouth full of half chewed toast.

"You didn't, or she didn't?" I swallowed and felt my temper start to flare up. I really didn't want to argue today so I took a breath and tried to keep my cool.

"Neither of us did. I didn't want a huge scene and Eren said it would feel wrong to do a big traditional wedding without Edward. So we're just doing this instead."

"Do you think she just said that to appease you?" she continued, poking the bear.

"No. She was the one who suggested it. Do you not want to come or something?"

"Of course I do. I'm sorry. I just wanted to make sure this was what you both really wanted."

I left the table and went to shower. I tried not to let her words make themselves at home in my head, but I could already feel them burrowing deep into my brain and setting up camp. The hot water beat down on my shoulders and I focussed on all the positive things Eren had ever said to me. She wouldn't have agreed to do things this way if she didn't actually want to, right?

I turned off the water and stomped back to the spare room where I'd laid out all of my things. I rustled around in my bag, looking for my phone and when I found it, I sat on the edge of the bed, glaring at it. I knew that if I rang her and heard her voice I would feel better but I didn't want to interrupt or worry her. I was in the process of tearing my hair out over the decision when, as if feeling my need for her, Eren made the decision for me.

"Morning, gorgeous, you okay?"

"Hey, I'm good. Are you?" she asked, sounding concerned.

"Okay seriously, how did you know? Are you a witch?"

She cackled down the phone at me, adding fuel to the mad accusation. "No, but your sister can't help but meddle so she told me that you might need me."

"That woman can't just leave things alone," I grumbled, mostly to myself.

"She's just trying to help. So what's up?"

I huffed and pinched the bridge of my nose. "It's just Flo, making me question things."

"Like what?"

"Like whether you actually want this," I all but whispered, irrationally terrified that saying the words out loud would make them true.

"Of course I want this. Why else would I have suggested we do it this way?" she told me, confused.

"Flo just got me thinking that you might be doing it this way to make me feel better." I heard Eren groan on the other end of the phone and a slight smile lifted the edge of my lips.

"I love your sister, Dylan, but God damn that woman needs to learn to stop talking! There is no other way I would want to do this. I just want our closest friends, your sister and my parents." She was quiet for a second and I could almost hear the cogs in her head turning.

"Are *you* getting cold feet?"

"No, not at all. I was just worrying about you, that's all."

Eren let out a sigh of relief, and I could picture her face in my head, her plump lips slightly parted, her eyes closed, the shadow of her lashes dusting her cheekbones and her hand running through her glossy blonde curls. The image had my heart racing but in the best possible way. I couldn't wait to be able to say that she was officially mine.

"Dylan, are you still there?" she asked.

"Yeah, I'm here."

"Are you good?" she asked, still an edge of concern in her voice.

"I'm great," I assured her. "I'll see you at the altar."

Her giggle was like music to my ears. "I'll be the one in white."

After my call with my future wife, I could barely contain myself. Marrying Eren had been on my mind for a long time, and now the day was here I was buzzing. It had become essential to connect myself to her in every way possible, and marriage seemed like the most sensible way to start. Just the thought of her having *my* last name and *my* ring on her finger was almost too much for my heart to handle.

Her friends walked through the door, sweet but knowing smirks on their faces as they greeted me at the altar. Layla threw a wink my way and I swallowed a laugh. I'd come to really enjoy both her and Angela's company, and I was glad they were able to be here for us.

Eren came into sight and I understood immediately why they had given me those looks. She was ethereal in white. I had to fight to keep myself in place so I didn't meet her half way down the aisle. Her parents were on either side of her, teary eyed and proud of their little girl. I briefly took notice of them but I couldn't keep my attention off the beauty in front of me. She was like a beacon calling me home, and when she finally met me at the front, my soul felt more at peace than ever before. Looking into her glistening eyes, I saw our future together. The blinding smile she gave me caused my heart to leap, and the realisation I would get to see that smile every day for the rest of my life brought tears to my eyes and a lump to my throat.

I'd never considered myself to be especially blessed. I'd been lucky in some ways, unlucky in others but now, with Eren by my side as my lover, my companion and my soulmate? Now, I was truly ready to live.

The End

Sneak Peek of Hope

by LAUREN GRACE

Neve

"Come on Neve, you're on stage in 5 minutes!" Reg, the bar owner, calls from the lady's bathroom door.

"Reg, I've told you before. You cannot rush me!" I yell back, leaning into the cracked and dirty bathroom mirror to add yet another layer of mascara.

I stand back and look at myself, my smokey eyes, my mass of hair falling in waves, my tiny black dress showing a hint of my red bra. I sigh. "It's just the beginning Neve, we all have to start somewhere," I remind myself in the mirror. I shut down my thoughts before I can think about how I've been doing the same gig for the past 18 months. How if it wasn't for Reg hiring me to entertain in his bar each week, I would be homeless.

"Ladies and gentlemen, please welcome on stage our girl, our little pop star. That's right. She made it all the way to boot camp on Popstar Superstar. Please give her a big hand."

"I'd give her more than that," a deep voice heckles.

"John, you're not big and you ain't clever. Keep your comments to yourself and while you're at it, you can keep it in your pants too. If what your ex-wife says is true, you actually have very little to give," Reg snaps back into the microphone.

I roll my eyes. "Jesus Christ, Reg," I mutter.

"Where was I? Oh yes, the fabulous Neve!" Loud music starts and I take a deep breath and open the door. Strutting on the stage, I smile and wave before picking up the microphone. I look out across the pub, and see the same few faces scattered about. The only one clapping is dirty Jon.

"Thanks for having me here tonight. I thought I would really get the party going as it's a Saturday night." The music for Tina Turner's Proud Mary starts up. I start singing and dancing around as best as I can on a small stage that is less than 6-feet in size.

The entire gig, I sing and perform as if I was

performing at Wembley or the O2 arena. I will forever give it my all as you never knew who could walk in and be your ticket to the big time. Even in the Golden Lion in Hounslow, you just never know.

After performing 5 songs, I take a break and head to the bar for a drink. "Usual please, Reg," I pant.

"Let me get that," a deep voice says beside me.

I don't even bother turning to face him. "Thanks, but no thanks," I answer, taking my water and walking away to sit at my table in the corner of the pub.

I flick through my phone, looking through social media, seeing people from school post pictures that are utter bullshit. The "look how happy we are" posts, with my amazing career and my 6-bedroom house. I wish there was a bullshit button, I would click that all day long. I mean, where are the honest posts? The posts that say, "I ate a fat kebab last night, I wasn't even drunk and it's the third takeaway I've ordered this week". Or when people with kids post about their perfect children, yeah well, we ain't buying that shit Brenda. The neighbours have seen your recycling bin and the 3 bottles of pinot. Yeah, we now your little angels are little shits, and your pinot is the only thing helping you to relax on an evening while you get five minutes of peace. And that's okay, because that is life and kids are evil!

"So who are you trying to hide from?" a deep voice asks.

I don't look up from my phone. "Who says I am hiding? Maybe I'm just avoiding people?" I state, taking a sip of my drink, still not looking up at him.

I feel the bench sink where he sits next to me. I sigh and roll my eyes. I still keep focused on my phone. I get enough guys who after a few pints think it is okay to try and chat me up, or grab my arse.

"Well, I suppose I never thought of the fact you could be avoiding people. So who are you avoiding?" he asks. "Could it be the guy who, I believe is sat there now scratching his under arm and I think he's about to–"

"Sniff it? Yeah, that's Tim. Give him another pint or 2 and he will start scratching and sniffing other parts of his body," I mumble, still scrolling through my phone, doing my best to try and ignore the guy sat next to me.

"Wow, now I'm not sure what to watch; you back on stage or wait and see what Tim scratches and sniffs next?" He laughs. "Okay, what about the guy with his wife?" he asks.

"That Walter and Julie, they are not married; well, to each other at least. Julie is married to Walter's brother and Walter is married to Julies best friend," I state.

"Wow, okay well, what about the guy in the leather jacket with worn jeans. Blonde hair that could use a decent cut, and I think a contagious smile," he asks.

I frown and look up around the bar. "There isn't anyone that comes in here like tha–" My words die in my throat as I look to the right of me and see the guy sat next to me. "You," I state.

He smiles, and he's right, he does have a nice smile. "And finally, she sees me," he mocks heartbrokenly.

I laugh. "So, are you going to introduce yourself or am I supposed to guess?"

He sits back. "Hhhm." He taps his chin. "Now there's a decision, tell her my name or keep the mystery going?" He pauses. "I think I'm going to let you guess, have at it," he gestures. Sitting back he winks at me.

I smile and shamelessly use this opportunity to look him up and down. He is no doubt my kind of guy. He clearly works out and those eyes and that smile. Damn. I lick my lower lip, looking up at him. I don't miss how his gaze drops to my mouth.

"I'm going to guess your name is Burt," I tease.

"Now, come on. You know that things that look this good don't come with a name like Burt." He winks.

Normally that kind of arrogance would put me off a guy, but with him it works.

"Fine, how about Steven?" I guess. He raises a brow. "Fine. Brody or Troy?" I ask.

"Jesus sweetheart, I ain't from fucking high school musical." He smirks.

"Well, I don't bloody know so why don't you just tell me?" I shrug.

"Now, where is the fun in that?" he quips.

"Neve, you're up in 5," Reg states. He looks to the mystery man. "He bothering you?" Reg asks.

"He's fine, Reg, no need to throw his arse out," I say standing before patting Reg's chest. "Yet," I add as I walk off towards the stage.

Acknowledgments

There are so many people that I need to thank for helping this book come to fruition. I couldn't have done this alone and I couldn't have survived this past year without the people below.

Firstly I want to thank Lizzie for taking a chance on me and having my debut novel be a part of your anthology series. I am so grateful for your support and your confidence in me. You are a complete and utter diamond and I'm so glad to have met you.

Heather, my angel, thank you for encouraging me and reminding me that I can actually do the things I set my mind to. Your advice and support has been invaluable to me, not just for this book but for every aspect of my life. You were the first person I told that I was writing and your enthusiasm for my stories have been a huge motivator for me.

Heleena, my best friend of a million years. Thank you for being my rock, my safe place and the person to tell me when I'm being a complete and utter nightmare. You have played such a huge role in my life, I don't know how to live without you and I have no intentions of finding out. Also, thank you for bringing me a baby to cuddle when I need snuggles.

Beccaaaaaaaa! You have been insanely good to me and I would have been a mess without you here telling me to shut up and get on with it. Your insight means so much to me and I love our chats. Thank you for caring so much about me, it's a privilege to be your friend.

Danny, my pasta princess, thank you for keeping me laughing whether I want to or not. Your talent for making everything fun is unparalleled and you are such a generous person with your time and your skills. I'm so proud to be your friend.

Jessop, thank you for being the kick up the arse I need when I want to give up. You are a writing machine and one day I hope I can be as focussed as you. So basically, I want to be you when I grow up.

Wendy, thank you for being an incredible beta reader. Your comments are so valuable to me and the way you see my work makes me feel like I'm doing something right.

My family, my boyfriend and my amazing friends, there are too many of you to mention individually. I know that I haven't been easy to love recently. Thank you all for dragging me through, kicking and screaming. I have no idea where I would be without you all.

My final thanks go to two men in my life. Simon, you're no longer here with us but I think of you every single day and I hope that you're proud of me. Your unconditional love and support meant more than I could have ever told you but I hope you knew. It was an honour to be considered your daughter. Theo, our newest addition to the family. Thank you for reminding me that good things can still happen, you have been my light in a dark place and I hope when you grow up you're proud to call me your auntie.

Printed in Great Britain
by Amazon